COLUMBIA COLLEGE
683.4G975C   C1   V 0
GUN PEOPLE$1ST ED.$GARDEN CITY N.Y.

3 2711 00004 5281

W9-DFL-361

GUN PEOPLE

LIBRARY
OF
COLUMBIA COLLEGE
CHICAGO, ILLINOIS
WITHDRAWN

GUN
PEOPLE

BY

Patrick Carr

PHOTOGRAPHS BY

George W. Gardner

A DOLPHIN BOOK
DOUBLEDAY & COMPANY, INC. GARDEN CITY, NEW YORK
1985

683.4 G975c

Gun people

DESIGN BY M FRANKLIN-PLYMPTON

Library of Congress Cataloging in Publication Data
Main entry under title:
Gun people.
    "A Dolphin book."
    1. Firearms owners—United States. I. Carr, Patrick.
II. Gardner, George William, 1940–
TS533.2.G86   1985   683.4'0092'2
ISBN 0-385-19193-6
Library of Congress Catalog Card Number 84-26014

Copyright © 1985 by Patrick Carr and George W. Gardner
ALL RIGHTS RESERVED
PRINTED IN THE UNITED STATES OF AMERICA
FIRST EDITION

For Christopher and Roberta

ACKNOWLEDGMENTS

We are grateful to all the people who consented to be portrayed in this book and gave us their time and their attention. Some of them were extraordinarily helpful, introducing us to their friends and colleagues in different areas of the country and fields of expertise, and to them we owe special thanks. They are Jerry Preiser and Paris Theodore in New York, Mike Dalton in Los Angeles, Jerry Thompson in Nashville, Dennis Peinsipp in Florida, and John Aquilino in Washington, D.C. Overall, two other people were absolutely crucial to our progress from start to finish: James Raimes, an editor who has it all and with whom it really is a pleasure to work, and Michael Bane, who introduced us to many of the people named above and was always there when we needed facts, background, and a real expert's advice.

INTRODUCTION

The United States is the only nation in the world which specifically grants its citizens the right to own and bear firearms. The Second Amendment to the Constitution declares that "A well-regulated militia, being necessary to the security of a free State, the right of the people to keep and bear arms, shall not be infringed."

That statement is notoriously open to interpretation, and the American citizen's right to "keep and bear arms" has indeed been "infringed," but the fact remains that a majority of Americans still possess the legal right to own a gun for hunting, recreation, or self-defense.

It is that last right, the private ownership of guns for personal protection, which is unique to the United States. While other nations often permit the ownership of firearms by farmers and hunters and sanctioned competition shooters, they all restrict the ownership of guns intended purely for personal protection to their military, their police and security agencies, and those upon whom the state wishes to confer special privileges.

In the latter half of the twentieth century, the American's right to self-protection with a gun has become a central issue in both the nation's perception of itself and the eyes of the world, and ever since the assassination of John F. Kennedy, the overall trend has been toward tighter control (or elimination) of the private citizen's legal access to firearms. Behind this trend is the notion that large numbers of guns in the hands of the citizenry encourage crime and deadly violence that would not occur without the availability of such instruments.

Recently, however, that notion has come under concerted attack, and is no longer the article of political faith it once was. The sweeping trend toward tough gun-control laws is now a hard-fought, bitter, and often unsuccessful campaign. The notion that we live in a society which is far from "civilized" and should act accordingly has risen to the fore, and more and more Americans of all political stripes are showing deep interest in the techniques of self-preservation. The national movement toward gun control, then, has become a loud and passionate debate of enormous political consequence, which is likely to grow still more intense and assume still greater importance in the political process at all levels of government.

The furor surrounding the debate is, in a way, responsible for the making of this book. The debate is so hot, and its issues so central, that it tends to be the only gun-related matter to which journalistic media professionals are willing to apportion time—which means that it is the only nonfictional gun-related information received by media consumers. Fictional input, of course, is available in megadoses—how *would* prime-time television sound without all those lively ripples of submachine gun fire, those manly shotgun blasts, the casual popping of .38s and .45s and .22s which keeps every plot line from "Dynasty" to "Hill Street Blues" moving right along?—but between these two extremes, between fear and romance, there is nothing: no nasty bang-bangs on ABC's "Wide World of Sports" to enliven the Saturday afternoon of America's 60 million bang-bangers, no "Lifestyles of the Armed and Interesting," nothing at all that calls for the depiction of real-life gun owners who have not recently shot somebody.

Obviously, there is a disturbing schizophrenia here, a strange and irrational divergence between the media's almost universally anti-gun journalistic coverage and its wholehearted fictional commitment to the gun as *the* power and glamour object, and the resultant middle-ground reality gap is communicated to media consumers. When the subject of guns arises during the average social conversation among nonshooters, the theme is almost invariably the gun-control debate—everybody, after all, can relate to mortal terror, especially when their local TV stations are constantly reminding them that it exists as long as anybody near them has a gun—while the shared pool of knowledge about gun lore, craft, technology, use, and the places guns occupy in people's lives, originates in the realm of the fantastic as presented by Hollywood. With such origins, this knowledge may or may not reflect reality with any accuracy, but it is all that is available through the media, and in a lot of places it cannot be checked by observation. In urban middle-class life, particularly, the few gun owners (typically cops and criminals) do not as a rule mix in polite society, so even this secondhand source of direct life experience is closed: the dominant ideology/imagery cannot be confirmed or altered (or, more to the point, expanded) by either hands-on experience or social contact.

In this context, it must be remembered that most media professionals were born to the urban middle-class life and almost all of them now live it; their social milieu is not the America in which guns are familiar objects of daily life, so they too are operating within a restricted-input scheme. Thus, the closed information circle is perpetuated: nothing new comes in, nothing new goes out.

It was this characteristic of media output, and the strength of the media-generated stereotypes available to me and those around me, that initiated my decision to embark upon *Gun People;* basically, I was curious. I wanted to find out who the "gun people" really were.

I sat down with that question, and began to make a list. It started, of course, with the categories that came most readily to mind from the local murder/blood-lust/mayhem-crime/war-and-craziness files available to me and my New York media colleagues: store owner who has shot somebody, angry New York pistol permit holder, cop who has been shot, SWAT team sniper, Florida machine gun store owner, NRA propagandist, paranoid person hoarding ammo in the sticks . . . But then I had to keep going, and I started coming up with categories like champion air-gun shooter, kid with a black-powder gun, genteel duck hunter, farmer with basic working guns, collector of fabulously expensive guns, foreigner delighted by the chance to play with guns,

gun designer, Yankee gun manufacturer, Civil War collector . . .

That was the point at which I realized that just like all kinds of other multipurpose inanimate objects, guns really did come with a whole society's range of humanity—the crazies, the humorists, the obsessives, the dilettantes, the scientists, the artists, the artisans, the philosophers, the men of action—revolving around them. Quite obviously, guns were not just for blowing away the opposition on the Lower East Side, satiating one's annual blood-lust for Bambi, or defending one's rural fortress against imaginary hordes of vicious inner-city dwellers.

The list of categories defined the scope of the book; all that remained was the method. That was very, very simple: *Gun People* demanded the "oral history" approach. The whole rationale behind the book stemmed from the fact that the voices of "gun people," if heard at all in the mass media, are routinely muffled by the louder voices of the editors, producers, and reporters presenting them, so the task facing George Gardner and myself would be to simply present those voices as clearly as possible, regardless of our personal opinions of what was being said. The copy in the book, therefore, should be in the form of first-person monologues edited from tape-recorded interviews. *Gun People* is not *about* gun people: It *is* gun people.

The Bureau of Alcohol, Tobacco and Firearms is the Federal agency charged with the duty of keeping track of firearms in the United States, and according to their figures, ownership of handguns stood at 24,700 handguns per 100,000 population in 1982. The figure for long-gun ownership, as one might expect, was greater: 53,700 per 100,000 people. The bureau estimated that in 1980, there were 50 million handguns in the United States, and that between 1974 and 1982, handgun ownership rose 25 percent, while long-gun ownership rose 15 percent. One gun does not necessarily imply one owner, of course—the typical gun owner has several firearms—and the best estimate of the number of gun owners in the United States comes from the National Rifle Association: between 50 and 60 million gun owners, 35 to 40 million of whom are handgun owners.

The BATF's figures do not indicate the intent behind ownership of these guns, but a private 1981 poll by Peter D. Hart Research Associates, Inc., of Washington, D.C., indicates the following breakdown for handguns only: for protection/self-defense at home, 51 percent; for target shooting, 12 percent; for hunting, 9 percent; as souvenirs or keepsakes, 7 percent; "just to own/just like a handgun," 5 percent; job-related, 4 percent; and for protection at work, 2 percent.

The most recent figures on geographical distribution of firearms, from the 1978 Decision Making Information Survey, showed an overall firearm ownership rate of 28 percent and a handgun ownership rate of 10 percent in the Northeast, rates of 51 percent and 24 percent in the Midwest, 66 percent and 39 percent in the South, and 45 percent and 29 percent in the West. These figures are in line with the geographical breakdown of gun control laws in the United States: strong gun control throughout the Northeast, diverse patterns of legislation in the West and Midwest, and very little legal impediment to gun ownership in the rural South.

Gun-control laws can be local, state, or federal. State and local laws in the United States vary enormously, from the virtually total ban on handguns in Washington, D.C., and many other large cities to the statute in Kennesaw, Georgia, requiring that an operable firearm and appropriate ammunition be kept in every household. One must remember, however, that federal firearms legislation applies everywhere in the United States, and that no community can go beyond the bounds of that body of law.

Federal law restricts the ownership of firearms and ammunition to U.S. citizens and legal permanent residents and denies ownership to felons, persons who have been committed to mental institutions, persons who use controlled substances, persons under indictment, persons dishonorably discharged from the armed forces, and persons who have professed allegiance to a foreign power or have advocated the overthrow of the U.S. Government. Everybody buying a firearm from a registered dealer in the United States must prove residence and fill out a form swearing that they fit into none of these categories. If they lie, they have committed a felony.

Federal law also forbids the direct mail-order sale of any firearm or the direct transfer of any firearm between residents of different states, forbids the carrying of any concealed gun in a public place without due authorization, restricts the ownership of certain types of gun (shotguns with barrels less than eighteen inches long, guns equipped with silencers, and others) to duly constituted law-enforcement personnel, and demands that people wishing to own fully automatic guns submit to intensive investigation, waive their search-and-seizure rights, and pay a fee of two hundred dollars per gun. Penalties for transgressing any of these laws are severe.

This is the backdrop for the national gun-control debate.

Obviously, there are a great many privately owned firearms (particularly handguns) in this society, and the gun-control advocates maintain that this fact is a direct contributor to high violent-crime rates and a high incidence of severe or fatal gun-related accidents. Their ultimate objective is a national handgun ban. The other side, led by the NRA, makes a crucial distinction between legally and illegally owned guns, and maintains that there is no positive relationship between high violent-crime rates and high legal-gun-ownership rates. They suggest, in fact, that the reverse may be true: that areas which feature large numbers of legally armed citizens also feature lower incidences of violent crime than do areas in which gun laws prohibit private ownership of guns suited to defensive purposes (that is, handguns). They also maintain that gun control laws already in force have not succeeded in reducing the incidence of violent crime.

In this debate, it must be remembered that both sides are arguing about people who are currently entitled to legal gun ownership; these people, if they bought any gun from a registered dealer since 1968, have already sworn that they are not criminals, mental incompetents, drug addicts, revolutionaries, or otherwise ineligible individuals according to the provisions of the 1968 Gun Control Act. Professional criminals—that is, the "repeat offenders" who are responsible for over 75 percent of the violent crimes that occur in this country—are already ineligible for legal firearm ownership and are, therefore, not the people against whom the gun control initiative is targeted.

The debate is rich in statistics, and the most essential of them come from the FBI. That agency began keeping track of firearms involvement in violent crime in 1974. Between that year and 1982, handgun ownership in the United States increased by 25 percent (and long-gun ownership by 15 percent)—but despite this fact, the FBI reports that overall firearm involvement in homicide fell by 11 percent during those years, and handgun involvement fell by 15 percent. Firearm involvement in violent crime overall (including homicide) fell from 34 percent to 29 percent. During that same period, National Safety Council figures show that the number of fatal firearm accidents fell from 1.2 per 100,000 population to 0.8. These figures do not support the notion that the proliferation of firearms leads automatically to an increase in their criminal or careless use.

Likewise, the figures on the differential between violent crime rates in strict gun-control localities and areas of easy firearm availability do not seem to support the notion that gun control decreases violent crime. In fact, violent crime rates are highest precisely in those areas, the large cities and the Northeast, where gun control laws are toughest, and lowest in rural and Southern areas where lenient gun-control laws are in force.

The international data on violent crime in armed and unarmed societies also pertain to the gun control debate. Overall, they show that in stable societies (that is, those not engaged in civil war or internal revolution), there seems to be little direct positive relationship between high numbers of firearms in the hands of the citizenry and high violent crime rates. Israel and Switzerland, for instance, have the highest number of firearms per household in the world (this because of both country's policies of universal conscription into the armed forces), but they have violent crime rates at the low end of the industrialized-nations spectrum. Japan and the United Kingdom, on the other hand, have extremely strict gun-control laws but comparatively high violent crime rates which are escalating rapidly.

The pro-gun-control advocates' interpretation of this phenomenon is that Israel and Switzerland are cohesive societies, while Japan and the United Kingdom are both societies in turmoil; this, they say, accounts for the violent crime differential, which would become even worse if handguns were made available to the citizens of Japan and the United Kingdom. Besides, they say, one cannot extrapolate from foreign statistics to the domestic issue.

The NRA's interpretation is radically different. They note that in Israel and Switzerland, citizens routinely keep a variety of the world's most effective antipersonnel firearms—assault rifles, submachine guns, fighting shotguns, and semi-automatic pistols—in their homes, yet the domestic violence rate is low. Assuming that people who live in Israel and Switzerland become passionately angry with their friends and family members much like people everywhere, they ask, does this not negate one of the opposition's central points—that the mere presence of a gun in the house initiates deadly violence that would not otherwise occur? They also cite U.S. statistics on this point: while overall gun ownership in the United States has risen by almost 60 percent during the last fifteen years, the domestic homicide rate has fallen by 11 percent.

The anti-gun-control advocates say that the situation in the United Kingdom is a blueprint for what is likely to happen in this country if privately owned handguns are banned. In the United Kingdom, private handgun ownership is restricted to a tiny minority—mostly public officials who are open to terrorist attack—and anybody else caught with a handgun goes immediately to jail for a number of years; these are laws with real teeth. Despite such tough laws, however, the criminal class in Britain has been arming itself with guns ever since the breakdown of the unofficial agreement between the police and the criminals in the 1960s, and incidents in which unarmed citizens face armed criminals are becoming commonplace; between 1972 and 1982, the number of robberies committed against unarmed citizens by a criminal with a gun rose 700 percent.

This, say the anti-gun-control advocates, is a clear indication that the extremely tough British handgun control laws do not work. These laws are the model for those proposed as federal legislation or already in force locally in the United States, and people opposed to their adoption make the point that if British criminals can acquire handguns in an island society that has been virtually handgun-free for fifty years, American criminals could certainly do no worse if legal handguns were banned. Following a handgun ban in this country, they say, law-abiding citizens wishing to protect themselves from criminals effectively would have to make a hard choice: provide themselves with an illegal gun (and thereby commit a criminal act), or cross their fingers and trust to the effectiveness of the police and courts in removing dangerous criminals from society.

If that choice had to be made, it would have to be made in the context of the violent crime rate in this country. In 1983, that rate stood at 555.3 violent crimes per 100,000 population, or approximately 1,122,000 separate reported incidents across the United States. That figure works out at approximately one violent crime per 180 citizens per year; the overall "real" figure is likely to be higher, since many incidents go unreported, and for people living in large urban areas the annual risk factor is anywhere from twice to ten times as high as one in 180. Over a ten-year span, therefore, a big-city dweller has between a 1-in-9 and a 1-in-1.8 chance of becoming the victim of a violent crime.

A crucial distinction made by the gun-control lobby is that between long guns and handguns. They campaign against handguns (which, being concealable, are much more suited to aggressive purposes), and say that citizens wishing to defend themselves in their homes can always do so with rifles or shotguns. On the face of it, this argument is unassailable—but anybody familiar with firearms use knows that it is not. Long guns, particularly in confined spaces, are unsuited for defensive use. They are heavy and hard to manipulate, and they involve powerful recoil and muzzle flash, which means that women and people of slight build or advanced age (precisely the people who most often have to resort to a gun in defense of their lives) cannot use them effectively. Also, rifle bullets, even if they hit their intended target, can keep on going, penetrating walls and doors and wreaking havoc well beyond the site of the shooting. Multiple-pellet shotgun loads are also dangerous; while devastating to the attacker, they can also be fatal to anybody (the shooter's child, for instance) who is near the intended target. Handguns have none of these disadvantages, which is why most people choose them for personal protection.

The statistics on how Americans use their legally owned firearms for self-defense is also pertinent to the gun-control debate. FBI figures show that in 1982, approximately 425 felons were killed by their intended victims in cases of "justifiable homicide." In 90 percent of these incidents, and in all of the cases where a woman was defending herself, the weapon used was a gun.

These were "worst case scenarios," incidents in which the shooter was forced to live with the social, legal, and emotional consequences of having killed another human being, and the deceased felon was denied access to the more conventional processes of punishment and rehabilitation offered by the criminal justice system; in these cases, the full and terrible consequences of defensive gun ownership were visited on both parties—but these cases must be placed in their proper context relative to the gun-control debate.

In this case, that context is the number of incidents in which people defended their lives or property with a gun, but with no fatal consequences. A large-scale random-sample survey by Peter D. Hart Associates reveals that over a five-year period ending in 1982, 9 percent of America's legal gun owners defended themselves with their guns against burglars, robbers, rapists, assailants, and would-be murderers. That figure works out at 1,735,000 incidents over a five-year period, or 347,000 incidents per year. In 1982, then, the approximate ratio of fatal to non-fatal gun defenses was (according to the FBI figure) 1 to 900. No matter how one looks at it, that ratio is extremely convincing on the issue of a firearm's deterrent value.

It is difficult to step back from the gun control debate, but I believe that some essential points about it must be made, and I feel compelled to make them. My position is that of the man in the middle; ever since beginning work on *Gun People*, I have been exposed to the arguments of both sides on a daily basis, and have become uniquely familiar with their ins and outs, and also their broader characteristics.

It must be stated here that the gun-control debate is not about the total elimination of firearms from our society, or the availability of guns to criminals, or the issue of gun-related accidents. Perhaps it *should* be about the two latter points—the institution of severe and enforced punishment for criminal gun use and of mandatory safety education programs for all legal gun owners might, perhaps, effectively address the two overwhelmingly obvious problems associated with firearms in the United States—but in fact, most of the energies of those involved in the debate are poured into one quite narrow question: the availability of defensive firearms (specifically handguns) to people who meet the criteria imposed by the 1968 Gun Control Act.

Given that, it seems to me that overall, the statistics favor the pro-gun forces, but those forces offer us a social scenario which is deeply disturbing. While their wish to see recreational shooters and responsible hunters take their pleasures without undue restriction is morally unassailable (except by animal-rights activists), the implications of their stance on handguns for personal protection are grim indeed: their relentless fight to guarantee the American citizen's right to defend his or her life with a gun implies that such an extreme is necessary in our society. That is a hard notion to sell to a nation which prides itself on its compassion. So, for the same reason, is their argument that what this country needs is not more restrictive gun control legislation, but a criminal justice system capable of removing the threat posed by violent criminals. Their basic point—that a national handgun ban would be nothing more than a placebo for the liberal sensibility—is a very bitter pill indeed.

The gun-control advocates, on the other hand, seem to offer little in the way of persuasive statistics, but the basic emotional appeal of their cause—Guns kill people! Get rid of the guns! Stop the killing!—is enormously seductive. One horrific incident of public mayhem like the "McDonald's Massacre" of 1984 is fully capable of winning literally millions of supporters to their cause despite the fact that it obscures the less newsworthy but no less brutal (and infinitely more frequent) daily violation of unprotected citizens in their homes across the nation; one photograph of a woman blown in half by her husband, when published in a national news magazine, provokes a clamor for gun control laws which ignores the fact that the woman would be just as dead with a dozen abdominal stab wounds or a skull crushed by a half-empty whiskey bottle—the techniques of choice in societies where guns are not available to private citizens. And in the United States, remember, a shooting is news; five stabbings are not.

The arguments, therefore, are very different in tone and implication, and it is the great irony of the debate (perhaps, given the resources expended on it, it is even a tragedy) that neither argument—one grimly pragmatic, the other heartbreakingly optimistic—can have any effect on the basic philosophy of its opponents.

In the end, the most essential questions of the debate often go unasked, or at least unconsidered by many of the people called upon to vote on gun control legislation. I think that those questions need to be stated here.

The first question is pragmatic, and the reader must answer it according to the data available at the time of decision. The question is, do gun-control laws (specifically bans on private handgun ownership) really work? Do they achieve their stated objectives—a reduction in violent crime rates, and a net increase in the security of noncriminal citizens?

The second question is moral, and to me it seems to be *the* moral question of the debate, especially if the answer to the first question is "No."

"Justifiable homicide" is a concept based in English common law and unchallenged in the history of the United States. A person has the right to kill, if necessary, when his or her life is threatened by criminal attack. Equally obviously, each citizen who is legally entitled to own a defensive firearm is free to make a personal choice about whether or not he or she is willing to do so in preparation for such a life-threatening eventuality.

The essential moral question, then, is this: if an individual does not wish, for whatever reason, to resort to the last line of personal defense represented by a gun, does that individual have the moral right to decide, by casting a vote, that nobody else should be permitted to exercise that option?

Now it is time to meet some gun people.

GUN PEOPLE

"I started doing less shooting in high school."

ANDREA COULEHAN, *an artist and mother who lives in Lenox, Massachusetts, shot a gun for the first time in fifteen years on the day she was interviewed.*

I began shooting at the age of about ten because the late Al Dynan took me under his wing. He was a top shooter in the Northeast, and he was also like a father to me.

We'd go out in the back and shoot his .45 whenever I was over at his house, which was frequently, and I really loved it. A gun is a very powerful thing, and as a kid, being able to shoot a gun was a big thing. None of my friends shot guns; they didn't do anything like that. I made bullets and everything, and I felt really good about that at that age.

I didn't really talk about it at school; it was just something special to me. And I was always outside, I was always sort of the tomboy of the family, so it was really natural for me to hook up with someone like Al, who didn't have any kids. He really liked showing me things, taught me how to drive his Jeep and stuff. He had hunting dogs, and I loved that whole life, I just thought it was wonderful. He was a country boy, very civic-minded, very bright, very compassionate. He had his own gun shop there in the house, and he had business from all over the country. Artie Shaw would come to the house, people like that. He made guns, too, and he was a hunter, and he would take me out hunting. He was a real sportsman, you know. He was a man's man. It was all very powerful, I thought back then. I still do. That type of man is always attractive to me.

At Al's funeral there were a few younger people who expressed the same kind of feeling for him that I have, so I think he had other kids he took under his wing. I never knew about anybody else at the time, though—I thought I was his little girl. I think I was, really. I really miss him now that he's gone, I really miss him. Still.

I started doing less shooting in high school, with boyfriends and activities and so on, and then I went away to college, and then I got married, and that kind of ended it. I just didn't see Al that much after that. But back when I used to go over to his house, he would really make sure that every time we would go out to the range in back and shoot. He really thought I had a lot of potential.

I never knew about this till later, but he talked to my parents about getting me into competition. They didn't want me to do it, though. I don't know why. I mean, they would let me go out on the range in back and shoot, so it wasn't as if they thought I was going to have a bad accident or something. It really doesn't make any sense. I wish that they'd let me. I just really don't understand why they did that. Pistol shooting at a target is just a great sport, and I really loved it. I was good at it, too.

When I shot just now, it felt great. It still feels great. I really started shaking after I shot those two shots because I haven't fired a gun in so many years, but I was still good!

"I average about three hundred per season when their fur is prime."

RAY MILLIGAN, *pictured with his three children and his Savage over-under .22/20-gauge combination gun, is a professional fur trapper based Santa Fe, New Mexico.*

During the late sixties and early seventies, the Vietnam years, my wife and I were part of the back-to-nature movement. We bought a small farmstead in north-central Kansas and had our three children there. My wife did pottery and weaving and stuff, and we had milk cows and pigs and chickens and ducks and goats, and I was a predator trapper. Then I wrote a book or two on trapping, and started to manufacture scent lures to attract wild animals. That business got going very well, establishing us nationally, and that afforded us the luxury to live anywhere in the country. We picked the Santa Fe area because it's a cultural hub, and because it's a very good area for trapping coyotes.

I chose coyotes because they are very destructive to livestock—their natural niche in this world is as scavengers, but when times are tough they become wolflike and kill sheep and even cattle—so landowners open their gates to me. Usually, access to land is the trapper's biggest problem.

Coyotes, in fact, have become quite a pest in recent years. Historically, they were a Plains animal, scavenging after the wolf packs which followed the buffalo, but something happened to them following the poisoning campaigns which ended in 1972. They dispersed, and now you find them everywhere. It's a phenomenon: nobody really knows why it happened, but we do know that coyotes are highly intelligent animals. We judge the intelligence of animals by the number of vocal sounds they make, and studies have shown that excluding primates, the wolf makes the most vocal sounds of any mammal. The coyote makes one sound less than the wolf, tying with the dolphin.

That makes them the hardest furbearers to put into a trap, but I do pretty well. I average about three hundred per season, when their fur is prime and they qualify as a renewable resource. They really are renewable, too. A female coyote is a very efficient and adaptable reproductive machine. If I go into a particular area and eliminate 60 percent of the coyote population, the females will react accordingly that year and produce large litters. If I hadn't gone in there, there would be less food per coyote and greater stress, and the females would react by producing smaller litters. I go back to the same farms every year, and every year I take eight or ten coyotes there.

I have no trouble selling the fur; the American fur market is growing these days because average Americans are beginning to realize that like the Europeans, they might never be able to afford their own house, but they can afford a nice car and they can afford a nice fur.

I take the Savage with me on the trap line. The .22 barrel will dispatch animals in the traps, and the 20-gauge shotgun barrel is for when they bust out of the traps, which they often do when you get near them. It's a simple gun without a lot of technology to go wrong, and I can depend on it. When it's twenty degrees below zero, or when I've dropped it in a river going after a raccoon, it will work.

4

"An inexperienced person with a gun in hand is more dangerous than a bear."

RON MCMILLAN *(with shotgun) runs the Bristol Bay Fishing Lodge in the Wood River lakes system of Southwestern Alaska.*

Up here we hunt anything from caribou and moose to ducks and geese, and of course there's bear. We've got quite a few Alaskan brown bears right around here. Some people call them "grizzlies," but any bear that's more than seventy-five miles from salt water is classified as "a grizzly," so you can call it what you want.

You have to watch out for them. Once in a while we'll get one come into the camp. Last fall, one came right up on the porch, and my wife had her nose against the window glass, looking out. The bear put his nose right up against hers, looking in. In the fall, I pretty much don't set foot outside the house without a gun, especially when I go out to turn off the generator for the night. It's pitch black out there, and you can run right into each other. People around here *always* have a gun handy.

This place here we call "Bear City." It's a place that people normally can't or don't get into, and there's a lot of salmon running in the river and lot of good berry bushes along there, so it's a good food source for the bears. There's high grass in there, and they'll lay up in it during the day-time. We fish there, and since I just don't want to walk up on one, before we go in I'll crank off a couple of shots to let them know we're coming. Usually they'll get up and look around, or they'll get up and run. These are very, very wild bears. They're not like the ones you run into in the lower forty-eight; these bears don't know people, so if they hear you talking, they'll leave.

I use a Ruger bolt-action .338 Magnum when I'm bear hunting, and I load it with 250-grain silvertips. For protection when we're fishing I use a 12-gauge pump or a .44 Magnum sidearm. I load the pump with Magnum slugs backed up by double-ought buckshot.

With the .44, let's put it this way: it's the most powerful handgun you can carry, with the muzzle velocity being what it is, so if a person had time to get it out, I think it could do a bear in pretty well at close range. I hope I never have to use it, though. I'd *much* rather use the shotgun. Still, it's a pretty mean handgun, and most people around here put a lot of faith in it being able to stop a bear at close range. Most of us who are carrying handguns are carrying a .44. The longer the barrel, the better. When you're carrying a lot of gear, sometimes you can't carry a shotgun too, so you have to rely on that .44.

We encourage our fishing clients *not* to bring any guns with them, because so many of them have the story in mind that every time they see a bear, they're going to have to use that gun. That's not true, and an untrained, inexperienced person with a gun in hand is more dangerous than a bear.

"A bird would come up, and subconsciously I'd shoot to miss."

SANDRA CIPOLLINO, *a New York State medical secretary, began shooting seriously three years ago. She competes in trap and skeet matches and hunts pheasant and deer.*

My first deer hunt was a strange experience. My husband had just gotten a .357/.38 combination Rossi lever-action carbine, which is a nice, light woman's gun in the woods, and we went out into the woods with it. I was standing there, and I saw this doe. We had a doe permit, so I put the gun up, but I got so nervous I said, "I can't do this!"

I put the gun down, and my husband said, "You dummy! What are you doing in the woods with a hunting license and a gun if you're not going to shoot it?"

So I picked the gun up, and I shot, and I got my first deer. Then it was like, "I don't believe I got it!" I didn't have any bad feelings then—it all went through my head before I shot. Once you've pulled the trigger, it's over. You either get it or you miss it, and *that's* what's important. That first time, it was so funny—I tell you, I never shook so hard in my whole life, about anything. The adrenaline rush is really something.

I guess I wasn't really sure about whether or not I was going to do it when I went out; it was the whole idea of shooting an animal, how to justify that to myself. It was like when I first started pheasant hunting. I'd be walking along, and a bird would come up, and subconsciously I'd shoot to miss. But I just had to make a resolve—either I started doing it, or my husband wouldn't take me hunting anymore—and understand that I was shooting them for food, that they weren't just going to waste. That's how I

justify it, and how I can enjoy it. And when you shoot your first one, and watch your own dog bring it back to you, it's really thrilling to see it all happen together. I can't really explain it, but it's so exciting, all of it. And I'm getting pretty good. If I get a chance to shoot at a bird, I don't miss.

I guess I'm the best woman shooter right around here, and in a lot of the trap and skeet matches we shoot, I'm the only woman. I've tried to get the wives of some of the men shooters into it, but they don't seem as interested as I am. It's like with women in general—I get some strong reactions when I tell them that I shoot. They find it totally amazing. They'll say, "You shoot?" Then they'll say, "Oh, I've always wanted to try it," and you say, "Well, try it! Come out and shoot!" But they don't. I guess they just don't think women should shoot. It's like a friend of ours who started shooting recently: his wife is so terrified by guns that when he built their house, he had to build a gun closet with a secret panel. She didn't even want to know what room the guns were in!

You get some men who are weird about women shooters, too. I applied for membership in a club around here, for instance, and it was approved by all but three of the men who had to sign it. I found out who they were, and went and talked to them. It turned out that they didn't want me in because they couldn't be "men" if I was there. They didn't feel that they could swear, and if they wanted to go to the bathroom outside they couldn't do that—you know, just be "men." What can I say? They all signed.

"The United States is a great training ground for terrorists."

RAY HAAS *is a counter-sniper and training officer with the Hillsborough County, Florida, Sheriff's Department Emergency Response Team. He is pictured with his ERT weapons.*

My ERT guns are a customized Colt .45 Government Model pistol, a lightweight M-16 assault rifle, a Remington 1100 12-gauge shotgun modified for combat use, and a Remington 700 sniper's rifle in .308.

The .45 is our personal weapon, and it's also the only gun we use in entry situations. A handgun allows you good reaction time and target selectivity, it's easy to reload, and the .45 round won't go through walls and hit your own people or civilians. Also, it doesn't have a long barrel; with a long-barreled gun, you run the risk of letting the bad guys know where you are, or having them grab the barrel as you go through a doorway. That's why our entry teams don't use shotguns; our shotguns are for firing gas shells and blowing the hinges off doors, that kind of thing.

We use the .45 because of the knock-down power of the .45 round. Once modified, the gun will put two very quick hits on the target, and will function perfectly 99.9 percent of the time; just like Ivory Snow, it's 99.9 percent pure.

My designation is "counter-sniper," and that's why I have the Remington 700. It does the job. It has a Brown's fiberglass stock, one of the first they made, and that keeps it at constant zero; I can put this gun away for a month, and it will shoot exactly where it always did when I take it out again. With this gun, I can make head shots at six hundred yards, and five out of eight body kill shots at one thousand yards. I put quite a lot of my own money into it, like I do with most of my equipment, but I'm dealing with people's lives here, and I have to trust my equipment.

Contrary to the public image of SWAT teams, we don't use the M-16s that much. The .223 round has very high penetration, so we won't use the M-16s in entry situations or in densely populated areas. They are for perimeter use, for assaulting buildings without entering them, and, should it ever come to it, for laying down a barrage of covering fire.

We've never had to do that in Hillsborough County. We've had to deal with disturbed people and bank robbers who were armed and holed up somewhere—in one case with explosives rigged—but we've never had a serious, professional problem with an organized group, hard-core terrorists. The closest thing to that in the United States is the biker groups. They're well armed and they train, and they could be effective.

Personally, I don't foresee too many immediate terrorist problems. The United States is a great training ground for terrorists—it's the only place where they can move freely, buy weapons, train with weapons, do whatever they want to do—and they don't want to ruin that situation by performing terrorist actions here.

That makes it easy for the people who don't want police departments to spend a lot of money on guys like us. They'll change their tune if a real problem does arise, of course, and then we'll all be playing catch-up with the terrorists.

"I think it's legal for me to have it, but it damn well ought to be illegal."

PATIENCE PIERCE *lives on New York City's Lower East Side. She owns only one gun, a Winchester .30-30 rifle.*

My ex-husband gave me this gun in New Orleans. It was on my first date with him. He gave me the gun, and he also gave me some diamond earrings. Then he took me out to dinner and we ate fish. Then we went to Sears and we bought bullets.

The first time we went to target practice, it was on a levee, and we were shooting at little Bud bottles, and I hit it right on the nose, first shot. I was an ace. And from then on I beat all the boys. Being a good shot was pleasing. It wasn't a surprise, though. I think it's easy. Guns are sort of like pool to me; if you can just *do* it and be very good at it in front of a lot of people, it's fun. I don't want to hurt or kill anything, but I do like it. I like to be good at it. I mean, who wants to be a shit at *anything*, right? It's better to be a natural.

I don't really know why David gave me the gun. Maybe he knew he was going to take me somewhere where I would need it. Maybe he thought he could impress me, show me that I was in for a lot more than just a romance. We did take a trip down the Amazon not long after that. That was our first trip together. It was a test.

In the city I hide the gun. I keep it in trunks, and I keep no bullets near it. It's hidden away. I don't want to be killed by some junkie with it or have to hit somebody over the head with it. Keeping it loaded would be *crazy*. I'd shoot myself with it, or some baby would shoot itself. Some innocent child visiting on Avenue B . . .

I think it's legal for me to have it, but it damn well ought to be illegal, 'cause it's a sharpshooter's dream out any New York window. I don't take it out and play with it or anything. If I did that, then I'd probably want to start shooting. See, that's the fear. The fear is that you'd want to start doing target practice, trying to find an empty lot in New York or something. Which would be just stupid, right? 'Cause it's only fun to shoot it. You want to shoot it. If you did, then they'd all pull out their little pistols and have a shoot-out.

They're always fighting out there on the street. It's very "drug" in the neighborhood. One time we came back from a tour and there were four men with rifles and Madras Bermuda shorts—they didn't really look like cops but I guess they were, some kind of special forces doing a drug bust—and that time we ran away because we were right in the middle. They were on either side of us, aiming right past us. But I hear shots all the time. One time we heard three shots, and we saw them take a body out of the heroin place down the block and put it in the trunk of a car. A couple of people died.

"I fired two warning shots—one in the lung, and one in the liver."

DR. RICHARD B. DROOZ, *a noted Manhattan psychiatrist and teacher, foiled armed robbers at both his office and his home before deciding to apply for a New York City pistol license.*

I am that rare individual, a New York City pistol-license holder. I came to be so after the second attempted robbery, in 1967. The commanding officer of the 19th Precinct police came over to inspect the shambles that my fight with the robber had made of my place before the cops finally showed up, said that he'd never seen such devastation, and asked me, didn't I have a gun?

I said no, I didn't have a gun, and he looked at me as if I were sort of crazy, and said, "Doctor, how long have you been living here in New York City?"

At his suggestion and urging I applied for my pistol license. After a year and a half of all kinds of delay and harassment and so on by the license division of the New York City Police Department, famous for delay and harassment, my license came through, and I've held it ever since.

I carry the gun when I'm abroad, out in the streets, and I personally believe that anybody who takes the trouble to obtain the license has a certain responsibility to have the gun available for the defense of himself and of other people. My own gun, I know, has served to help some other people besides myself.

Incidents do happen. On one occasion, I was driving back to the office late one morning. My teaching work is in Brooklyn, in the heart of the most crime-ridden area of New York City, and I was stopped behind a line of cars at a light. As the car at the head of the line started to move out, while I was still obstructed from the front, the door of my car was suddenly ripped open, and a young man pointed a gun at my head and threatened to kill me. He was backed up by two others, one with a knife and the other with what was apparently a toy gun.

I had my gun cross-draw under my coat, and I drew and fired. As I like to tell it, I fired two warning shots—one in the lung, and one in the liver.

The young man in question did not die, although he made a deathbed confession. I must tell you that subsequently, he was extremely nasty to the hospital personnel, and threatened to come back after his release and burn the hospital down. A suspicious fire did in fact start at the hospital shortly after his release, and I received a rather crude message from the staff, the tenor of which was "Why didn't you kill the sonofabitch?"

The gun I carry, and the one I used in the incident in my car, is a .38-caliber Chief's Special, stainless "snub-nose." I have other guns, but this one, being a small revolver, is a comfortable gun to carry. Also it has a special sentimental attachment because it came from a lovely man, a very prestigious firearms dealer who was prominent in religious and community activities. One day his store was entered by a man out on parole from Elmira State Reformatory, who just in cold blood killed him and gave his brother a depressed skull fracture.

"I want people to know I have it."

DEANNE PETERSON *works as a bartender on the* Queen Mary *in Long Beach, California while studying international politics. She owns a .38 Special Smith & Wesson revolver.*

I got the gun when I moved from Grand Rapids, Michigan, to Chicago. I felt that having it gave me a necessary sense of security. I took my father with me to get it. He knows all about guns, so it was like having my own in-house expert. We wanted to make sure that it was a gun I could handle, but that it would stop an intruder, which is what it was for.

It's pretty, huh? I keep it all shined up. It's a fun little gun to shoot; it has enough of a kick that I feel like I'm really shooting a *gun,* it isn't like a .22. They tried to talk me into an automatic, but I didn't feel comfortable with it. When I pull this trigger, I feel like I really have to pull it to get the gun to work. And it's easy for me to load.

When I came here from Chicago I didn't bring it with me at first. I *knew* I shouldn't bring it on an airplane. But then I went back for my furniture, and brought it with me. Once I had it, you see, I didn't feel safe without it. I go out to the range and shoot it about, oh, once a month. I keep it loaded with hollow-point bullets.

I'm very open about having the gun. I want people to know I have it. I would hate to have my friends think they're going to pull a prank on me and crawl in my window some night, and have me shoot them. People do like to pull pranks, and I seem to have friends who have that kind of a sense of humor . . . Otherwise, people are curious about it. They want me to take it out so they can look at it.

I keep it in my bedroom, but I move it from place to place in there. Sometimes it's under the bed, sometimes it's in a bookcase, sometimes it's in a drawer. I used to keep it in my lingerie drawer, of course. That's where women always keep a gun, right?

We had a Peeping Tom here, so I got the gun and cocked it and told him I had it, and I would use it. I'm more frightened of having someone grab me than I am of shooting someone. I didn't go to the phone and call the police; I know from experience that they don't respond as fast as you'd like them to in a crisis.

See, my first reaction was that I was *really* angry. I mean, you have to make a definite effort to look in these windows—there are bushes, and there's iron out there—and I knew that we'd never feel as safe as we once did in here. The guy left, but I walked around in here with the gun in my hand for hours.

In a way, my attitude frightened me, because I knew that had he come into the house, I would have shot him.

But really, the minute I know someone's in the house, I'm yelling, "I have a gun, and I'll shoot you!" And if they don't hightail it back out, that's as much of a threat as I need. I *really* don't want someone in my house that doesn't belong. I know I could be in trouble with the law if the person isn't armed, but I'm not real concerned about being convicted and sent to jail. Being a young female of two females living alone, I think I'd get off pretty lightly.

"This guy came out of a closet with a double-barreled shotgun."

TOMMY WALKER *has worked as a professional boxer, a bodyguard, an actor, and a children's magazine publisher. He is pictured in his Chicago apartment with his brother's .32 H & R revolver.*

I've had to use guns a few times. They've saved my life.

I used to go collecting rent for this guy, and there was attempted robbery on me a couple of times. I used to wear a lightweight .38 Detective Special stuck in the back of my pants. One time this cat was shooting at me with a .22, so I got off a shot. Nobody got hurt, and it was cool.

Another time, I was in a foreign country, and things jumped off. There was a minister, myself, and some other people, and I was one of the people they were relying on. Basically, everybody was starting to lose their heads, and there were some people with handguns who were trying to stop us getting across to the other side where there was a plane waiting to take us away. I can't say that I hurt anyone, but I did get off enough rounds so that I got the people from the mission across and into the plane and to safety. I'll say this much: it was the Congo.

I've gotten a few bullet wounds. I've got spots on my arm and in my side here, where I was shot with a shotgun when a person was trying to rob me. At the time I had a Walther P38 on me. There was a lady from Arkansas that was twenty-seven years old and had eight or nine kids, and I used to go to the building with food for the kids. Well, this lady had a nephew who laid around on his ass and didn't do nothing, and he knew I carried money, and one night he arranged for his friends to rob me.

So I was sitting on the couch with a kid between my legs, playing with the kid and talking to the lady, and this guy came out of a closet that had a curtain in front of it, and when he came out he had a double-barreled shotgun. He said, "This is a stickup. Take out all your money and your jewelry and give me the dough."

I said, "Man, you're crazy. You're pointing that gun, and this kid is here!" All the time I was thinking that this guy was going to hurt me, because he was shaking. I had the P38 on my left side under my suede jacket, and the safety catch was on, so I was trying to figure out what to do, because this guy *was* going to hurt me.

I said, "Man, c'mon, let me move this kid," and I raised the kid up and got my jacket up and knocked the safety off, and I pushed the kid away.

We were in a basement, and there was a pipe there with insulation around it, so when he fired the first barrel, all that white shit went in my eye, so I thought he'd blown my face open.

I rolled around and came up and got two shots off. The first one hit him in the leg and ricocheted up his hip, and the second one hit him in the side. He fired the second barrel into the wall. I went over and put my stuff to his head and flushed his cousin out, and somebody called the cops, and thank God, one of the cops who showed up knew me pretty well. The kid with the shotgun went to the hospital and he was all right, and the thing stayed off the record.

The bullet wound I got here in my leg was from a lady who decided that she liked me a lot and I was unfair to her. She came in and emptied a .22, but only hit me once. I didn't even know I'd been hit until I got in my car—I was pretty nervous—and felt the blood in my shoe. The round had gone into the bone and flattened out.

"Where that red dot is, that's exactly where the bullet is going to go."

JIMMY QUENEMOEN AND SUSAN SNYDER *live in Clearwater, Florida, where Susie runs a surplus store and Jimmy a diversified security business. Susie is pictured with an AR-15 assault rifle equipped with various sophisticated sighting systems, and Jimmy demonstrates the art of rappelling forward off a building roof.*

SUSIE: We built the buildings we have here—a chartreuse house, a purple-and-white house, and an orange-and-green camouflage house—and we're pioneers. It's an all-black neighborhood, and we are the only people who would have the nerve.

Of course, the people in the neighborhood know us, and know who we are, and we don't get any trouble at all. Nothing—not even bottles or chicken bones or anything thrown into the property. The local cops know us too. Sometimes we go up on the roof of the building at night with the AR-15 and the laser sight, and sight in on the police cars. Those guys see that little red dot show up on their car, and they know: "Oho, that's Jimmy!"

JIMMY: That's a great weapon. The AR-15 is a great little rifle, and the sighting systems make it just about unbeatable. That's the state of the art, right there. The laser on it projects a beam which puts a red dot on whatever you're aiming at, and where that red dot is, that's exactly where the bullet is going to go, right there in the middle of that red dot.

That particular type of laser has an interesting history. It was originally designed for the American 180, which is a drum-fed, two thousand-round-per-minute full-auto .22 built for police departments. It was a psychological thing; they wanted to bring it out and let the press hear about it, let it be seen on television, so that the bad guys would know what it was. If you were holding a hostage, and you saw that little red dot on your chest, you would know what was going to happen if you didn't surrender. In three seconds your chest wouldn't be there.

Police departments didn't go for it, though. They thought it was a cruel weapon, basically. I mean, you can put that dot on a cinder-block wall with the American 180, and just cut it in half. It's like a buzz saw. Unbelievable. Small targets are just gone, vaporized.

With the laser on the AR-15, though, sometimes you don't even need to put the weapon to your shoulder. When I'm running assault courses, I can run into a building with four or five targets seven yards away, put the dot on the targets, squeeze the trigger a couple of times for each target, and just buzz right through that building. You don't have to stop or anything—just do it at a dead run, because wherever that dot is, that's where your bullets are going. It totally eliminates the business of lining up your rear sight and your front sight and the target, and it totally eliminates guesswork.

"At night you can find the target with the Starlite scope."

SUSIE: The laser's only part of it, though. That gun also has the Aimpoint sight, which is like a conventional scope except that instead of cross hairs it has a little illuminated red dot in the center of the sight. Then it has the Starlite scope, too. That's a light-amplification sight; you can see at night with it. At night, you can find the target with the Starlite scope, get the red dot in the Aimpoint centered right on him, then flick on the laser and put that red dot right on him. Then, if you want to shoot, you've got him. And if you don't want to shoot, he knows you can.

JIMMY: The whole system is fairly expensive right now—though it's like pocket calculators and stuff, the price is dropping fast—but even so we sell quite a few of them. Mostly we sell to people with boats. Anywhere in the Florida area, you see, you have a problem with hijackers; the drug smugglers need lots of boats, 'cause they usually sink them when they've made one run with them, and usually they kill everybody on board when they do a hijack.

People with big boats will buy a Starlite and a laser, then, and mount them on an AR-15 or a Mini-14. That way,

they can eliminate a very serious problem without even firing a shot. The people who are going to hijack them know what it is when they see that red dot on their boat, and when they see an AR-15 or a Mini-14, they know that those guns will punch holes in half-inch steel at seventy-five yards. So they just leave, see.

I've seen boaters come in who are totally against guns, but the fear has overpowered them, they just have no choice. They'll buy the gun and they'll buy a couple of thousand rounds of .223 ammunition, they'll go out to the range and practice, and they'll put it on board. They have to.

SUSIE: Really. It just started a few years ago, and it happens all the time. That laser and the AR-15 are a real good deterrent, though.

It works pretty well around here, too. Jimmy gets out of his truck here with it, and probably a .45 too, and people know. They know Jimmy. He's a locksmith, and he's the only one who will go in this neighborhood after dark. They call him "Magic Jim."

"Happiness is a belt-fed weapon."

DENNIS M. PEINSIPP, *a Vietnam veteran, runs Shooter's Shak, Central Florida's largest firearms dealership, and Counterforce Special Security, Inc., in Clearwater. He is pictured with a standard U.S. military machine gun, the M-60.*

The M-60 machine gun is my favorite weapon. It's belt-fed. It hooks up to an ammunition belt, and it just flat gits it—twelve-hundred meter range, .308 caliber. That's the way to go to war! Happiness is a belt-fed weapon.

It has to be belt-fed, see, because the machine guns you see on TV—you know, this little thing the guy has in his coat—are submachine guns, and they don't make it unless you're going to murder someone in a phone booth. That's because the average submachine gun has a cyclic rate of between seven hundred and nine hundred rounds a minute, but it only has a thirty-round clip.

What that means is that you have somewhere between one and a half and two seconds of firepower before your clip is empty—zzt-zzt, it's over!—and the average trooper ain't bright enough to pick a target, shoot the target, and move on to the next one in that amount of time. The only full-auto that's worth a shit in the field, then, is a belt-fed weapon with a lot of ammo.

They found out about all that the hard way in Vietnam by giving everybody a full-auto weapon. That wasn't a smart thing to do. Most of the guys were going zzzt, zzzt, and not even hitting anything, and there went twenty rounds. I think the number of rounds expended per kill in Vietnam was something like seventeen million. In World War II, where the guys had to aim, I think it was something like one-point-two million. That tells you something: you can't hit nothing if you don't look down the sights.

That was a mess in Vietnam, though. The new standard rifle, the M-16, was thrown into a combat zone without proper testing, and so it had problems all by itself. On top of that, the military took guys and trained them on the M-14 in the United States—made 'em sleep, live and die with this big, heavy hunk of machinery you could use as a baseball bat—and then put 'em on a boat, handed them an M-16 at the other end, and said, "Go to it, bozo-breath. Go kill some gooks."

The guys looked at this thing, and it looked like a toy. It was full-auto, it was all this plastic stuff, it was half the weight of the guns they'd been trained on, it had half the range of what they'd been trained on, and it shot a bullet that was half the size of what they'd been trained on. These guys didn't even know how to load the magazines properly.

So the M-16 got a bad reputation it didn't deserve, and you still hear that around today. But most of the young kids coming out of the Army today, they love that 16. I do, too —always have. You hear a lot of bitching from people who don't know any better about the capabilities of the .223 round it fires, but have they ever seen what it does?

It's that light bullet and those high velocities. We had an ARVN in our group in Vietnam who was shot in the back of the leg with a .223: the round went into his leg, came up across his body, and came out behind his ear. If he'd been shot with an M-14, he might have lost a kneecap.

That round had a lot more killing power than anyone ever credited it with, until the Russians adopted it. Then it was just dandy. That's kind of funny; the Russians accepted it, so it must be good. You hear a lot of that kind of crap in my business.

"The Carcano was a fake-out, a cover-up gun."

RUSH HARP, *a pneumatics and firearms expert, described himself as an "assassinologist" for the last one third of his life. He is pictured with a Carcano Mannlicher rifle, the type of gun said to have been used by Lee Harvey Oswald. Mr. Harp died suddenly in Woodstock, New York, some three weeks after he spoke to us.*

The second day after JFK's assassination, I knew there was a conspiracy, because the cops in Dallas had signed an affidavit saying that the gun used was a 7.65-millimeter Mauser with a 4-to-3× 'scope, and they had identified it absolutely. I figured that was right, because a Mauser would blow Kennedy's head off, because it's some gun, it's equivalent to our .30-06. Then, the second day—*oho!*—it was a Carcano Mannlicher like this one here, and hey, they had made a mistake. Now it was a 6.5 millimeter, and I said "No way!"

Then I noticed that in the description of the Carcano, nobody had found the clip. A Carcano Mannlicher will not function or repeat without a clip. With a Carcano, you push the loaded clip down into the gun, and as you work the bolt and fire five rounds, as the sixth round goes into the breech the clip falls out the bottom of the gun; there's nothing to hold it in. But there was no clip in the gun, near the gun, found by the gun. There were three empty shells and one live round, which was still in the gun. That should have left two more live rounds in the clip, and the clip in the gun—but there was no clip, and no other live rounds. There were other mistakes, too, about where the empty shells were and what kind of 'scope was used, and also, we have a picture of the Mauser, after it was found, being held up on the roof of the Texas School Book Depository Building by the police. That was in the Dallas Cinema Association movie. So we know that the Carcano was a fake-out, a cover-up gun.

In fact, Kennedy was hit by four bullets. First, someone in front of the sign (this is all as seen in the Zapruder film) gets him in the neck with an umbrella gun from a range of about five yards. The idea of that was to paralyze him. I've got one of the rockets that are fired from the umbrella gun. I bought it at a gun show. It was a weapon designed for the CIA.

So in the Zapruder film you see Kennedy reaching for his neck; that's the puncture wound done by the rocket fired from the umbrella gun. Nobody carries an umbrella in Dallas, but in the film, on this nice sunny day, this guy whips out an umbrella when Kennedy comes along, and rotates it, aiming at the limousine, and—ah!—Kennedy's reaching for his neck.

He stays paralyzed for the next one hundred frames of the film, then three bullets hit him within two frames. A pistol bullet hits him in the back at frame 312, and his head goes forward two inches, and then at frame 313 he explodes, because a shot coming in from over his cheekbone blows out the right side of his skull, and a shot coming from the Grassy Knoll blows out his occipital bone. My guess is that those two shots came from .30-06-type rifles firing scintered uranium bullets, which weigh sixty percent more than lead bullets and are totally frangible. That's why, in the X rays of Kennedy's brain, you have thirty or forty "stars," which are little tiny bits of metal. No normal bullet is going to do that.

"We Japanese are always fascinated to see guns."

ROCKY AOKI, *the multimillionaire owner of the Benihana restaurant chain, has been a champion wrestler, power-boat racer, and intercontinental balloonist. He is pictured in one of his homes with part of his gun collection.*

I used to collect guns. I collect anything. I have Indian art, I have Japanese and oriental antiques. I collect stone statues—I love stone statues—and I have many lions' heads in the house and outside too. Right now I have maybe five Ferraris and eighteen Rolls-Royces of all kinds. I used to collect restaurants, too—French restaurants, Indonesian restaurants, other kinds of restaurants—but then I changed to just collecting Benihanas. I also used to collect antique Japanese guns; then I started to shoot, so now I have old guns and new guns too.

But I don't collect all these things anymore. I have so many things that I don't want to own anything more. Talk about airplanes? I have four different kinds of airplane, and I don't even fly. I have a pilot sitting in the Miami house doing nothing, because I don't fly. I don't want to waste my time and money, so I don't collect things anymore.

That's why I didn't renew my New York gun permit. As a matter of fact, I had a permit to build a pistol range in the garage, but the garage burned down, so everything went kaputo.

I used to carry a small gun on my leg, though, inside my boot, because I'd rather kill a guy than have him kill me. When I had just three restaurants in New York, I collected cash from Benihana West, Benihana East, and Benihana Palace—but since I don't see the money anymore, I don't have to carry a gun. I have a driver to pick me up and take me anywhere I want to go, so I am very safe.

Back when I had a smaller operation, I wanted to protect myself. If somebody stuck me up, I would have been the first guy to give everything I had: that's why I used to wear a lot of gold around my neck and on my fingers—to have something to give. I thought of the gun in the same way: if something happened, I wanted to survive, I wanted to live. I have survived so many accidents—in my car, in my boat, even an airplane crash a long time ago—so I know about surviving, and now I feel that I can survive without the gun.

I like small guns because I am small. The gun I used to carry was a Browning .25 automatic. It shoots well, that gun. It's very powerful. It hurts a little bit, but it's a challenge: with a small gun, you have to have a technique to shoot well.

In Japan, all guns are prohibited. Only policemen have guns. That's why we Japanese are always fascinated to see guns. One of the reasons I collected them was that fascination. In Miami, you know, you can just buy a gun if you are a legitimate person and you have the right identification. It's amazing. Now, I have over a dozen guns: back in Japan, I never even saw them.

Lots of Japanese friends of mine come over here, and the first thing they want to do is shoot. It's the first time in their lives that they've shot a gun! It is such a pleasure for them.

"It reminds me of the pioneer days."

RICHARD THOMPSON, *twelve, lives in the country outside Nashville, Tennessee. Like a growing number of shooters, he specializes in muzzle-loaded black-powder guns of the type used by early American settlers.*

I first started shooting when I was about nine, shooting a .22 Magnum with a scope on it. Our neighbor, Bob Mann, taught me how to shoot down there by the back pond. Then that Christmas I got a .22 single-shot rifle, then I shot my mother's .30-06 that she got from her grandfather, and then I got a .410 shotgun from my daddy that he used to shoot. Then I got my black-powder guns; I got the newest one, the long gun, for my birthday back in March. So first I shot modern-type guns, then black powder, and I don't believe I'll ever shoot a modern gun again.

It's an awful lot of fun to shoot black-powder guns, 'cause you don't have but one shot and you have to make it count. It reminds me of the pioneer days when all the people had to use guns like that against the bears and Indians and all. I like to learn about those days. In school, in Independent Studies, I did the history of gunmaking, and then just last Saturday we had the Scoutarama, and we made guns there using the *Foxfire* books. I took all my guns up there and showed 'em.

Black-powder guns are real fun to hunt with, 'cause it's a real challenge to kill something with a black-powder gun, especially my 12-gauge shotgun. You have to do a lot of work to get it loaded and ready to fire, and then when you've shot it once you have to do all that again. My shotgun is a caplock, too, and it's real hard to keep your aim when the primer in the pan goes off before the charge in the barrel.

I'm pretty good with it, though. My friend down the road hunts too, with a modern 20-gauge pump shotgun, and I killed more game than him this year—quail, rabbit, dove, squirrel. With the black-powder shotgun, you can put in two charges of shot if you want to, and you can also judge your loads for each shot instead of having to reload your own shells; in that way it's just as good as a modern shotgun, and it's a lot lighter, too. The modern guns have pumps on them and stuff, and that makes them too heavy for me. I might be able to get good with a modern 20-gauge, but not a 12-gauge. None of my friends shoot black powder—they all shoot modern guns—and I'm about the youngest person around here with black-powder guns.

One of the bad things about black-powder guns, though, is that every time you shoot you have to wash 'em out with soap and water, then let 'em dry out and then oil 'em real good, or they'll rust. That must have been hard for the soldiers and all in the old days. They'd have to get the water out of the creek and heat it up. Often they didn't wash them out—they just let 'em rust.

This is a good area for history. We're doing "Historic Trails" at school, and the Trail of Tears ran somewhere right through here. About a hundred yards from here, down in the woods, there are three mounds, and we think they're Indian graves. We did an archaeology unit in school, and I'm gonna dig them up sometime. If I find anything, I'll call the university and give it to them.

"You ask a kid, 'Do you want to go shooting?' It's, 'Oh, yeah!' "

MARSHA BEASLEY *is a U.S. Champion smallbore rifle shooter and is Junior Programs Coordinator with the National Rifle Association. She works to develop and promote youth shooting programs in the United States.*

In competitive rifle shooting, it's not so much the amount of time you put into it as the quality of the time. It's been said by several top coaches that how fast you progress is directly related to your ability to analyze your shooting, to think about it. This is in contrast with a sport such as weight lifting, in which somebody who does enough lifting and strength training—practice—will progress. In shooting that's not true; it all hinges on how well you think about what you're doing.

People have varying natural talent for shooting, of course, but it is a sport which can be learned. All you have to have is correctable eyesight. Then you have to learn how to hold the rifle steady enough to shoot a ten, you have to learn how to read the wind, and you have to develop the mental skills—basically concentration—to be able to repeat each action time after time in a match situation. Once you do all that and you get really good, you're basically shooting for perfection: in the standard .22 rifle prone event, where you shoot sixty shots at a ten ring less than half an inch in diameter fifty meters away, the world record is a 598 out of 600. There is just no room for mistakes.

More women are getting involved in shooting, partly because three Olympic shooting events for women were added for 1984. Also, the NRA is looking for ways to make the sport more accessible to females. Right now, the aver-age junior program has about 20 percent females—but why is that? Is it that girls don't want to shoot, or is it that they've always been *told* that they don't want to? We would like to move it closer to fifty-fifty.

This is a great sport. It offers opportunities most other sports don't. As I said, it requires learned skills and doesn't depend on body size or weight or strength. Shooting is a very safe sport. Additionally, it's not one you have to abandon when you turn sixteen or thirty; it's very much a lifetime sport. It offers team camaraderie as well as solo competition, and in addition to sport, develops great things like discipline and concentration, that kind of thing.

There are about two thousand NRA-affiliated Junior Clubs, which is how most young shooters get their start. I started shooting at age eleven at a junior club, but if there hadn't happened to be a club four blocks from my parent's house, I doubt I would have ever gotten involved in the sport. I'd like to see clubs that offer youth shooting programs in every community in the United States, so that every kid growing up would have the chance to learn to shoot.

It is a shame there are not more adults interested in organizing junior clubs, because I think that kids are almost innately interested in learning to shoot, or at least trying it. If you ask youngsters, "Do you want to go shooting?" without exception it's "Oh, yeah!" That's how it's been with every kid *I've* ever asked, boys and girls too. People just love to shoot, and they really should get the chance.

"IPSC shooters are the most proficient gun handlers in the world."

Mickey Fowler *progressed from motorcycle and automobile racing to International Practical Shooting Confederation and NRA "action shooting" competition. He is a three-time Bianchi Cup winner and a U.S. National Combat Champion.*

The appeal of the sport is that whereas most formalized handgun competitions use the same course of fire every time, with the same point total to shoot for, IPSC shooters are constantly given new challenges; it's a new match with a different course design every time. This means that IPSC shooters are the most proficient all-around gun handlers in the world. They learn it all: how to draw the gun quickly, how to hit a small target quickly, how to reload the gun quickly, how to shoot running, sitting, strong-handed, weak-handed—whatever—from all kinds of positions at all kinds of ranges. A world-class IPSC shooter can't have a hole in his skills.

The word "practical" is in the name of the sport because the sport is somewhat related to real-life self-defense with a handgun. Some of the matches are built around simulated real-life situations that could actually happen. You shoot at cardboard, buff-colored targets which simulate a head and torso, the aim being in most cases to place two quick shots in a vital zone, and there are no restrictions on equipment; you use whatever you think is going to do the best job. The equipment we use nowadays, therefore, is a direct result of match design. A lot of the guns, for instance, have compensators. That's because compensators cut down on muzzle rise, which means that your second shot can be fired accurately a lot more quickly than it otherwise would. That also means, of course, that the guns we use in competition are not practical guns for self-defense; not many people would want to carry around a gun that has as many gadgets on it and is as long as a compensated .45 Government Model.

Even though the sport is called "practical" shooting, then, it's basically a game. It flies completely in the face of sound self-defense tactics much of the time. If you used the tactics that win IPSC matches in a real-life self-defense situation, you'd be in a lot of trouble. On the other hand, the game does teach you to shoot a powerful handgun quickly and accurately, and that is no small advantage.

The game really started catching on in a big way in the middle 1970s, and since then it's grown a hundredfold, with all that entails. When I got started, the most you could hope to win was a gun; now, it's possible for a top shooter to win about fifty thousand dollars a year, plus equipment and contracts with gun and accessory manufacturers. The future of IPSC or "action" shooting lies with companies outside the firearms industry, though; if it really takes off, it'll be because cigarette and beer companies and the like get involved. We're starting to see that now, and also some regular media coverage. We're bucking a very strong anti-handgun media bias, of course, but hopefully, while the sport has a way to go before it achieves the dollar status of golf or tennis, it can surely get up to where you can be a full-time professional shooter.

"After a while, shooting becomes the only thing that's interesting."

MICHAEL BANE *began his journalistic career as a newspaper-man. Innumerable article and book credits later, he now freelances out of Tampa, Florida.*

I started shooting when I was about six. I shot with my father, and when I got older I went out shooting with my friends. That was in Memphis, and in Tennessee in those days, it wasn't that big a deal to shoot. You'd just go on down to any vacant lot and plink away; nobody thought that much of it.

When I went to college, then, it was a real shock. I got a job on the college newspaper right away, and on the first day they explained to me that to have the right attitude, you had to be "for gun control." Back in Tennessee, that attitude was nonexistent.

It was funny. I still had guns, but this was college in the sixties; I had a ponytail, the whole deal. People would come out to my trailer, look around, and say, "What's that?" I'd say, "That's a gun," and they'd go, "Oh my God! It's a gun!" Eventually I got a Huey P. Newton poster with the quote "An unarmed people are slaves, or subject to slavery at any moment." I'd just point to the poster, and that was okay: if Brother Huey says it's cool . . .

Having guns where other people didn't, and having guns but having no decent place to shoot them, continued until just a couple of years ago when IPSC-style combat pistol shooting started up here in Tampa. I was desperate to shoot, so I got involved in that, and for the past year or so I've been doing it really seriously. I tried to do it haphazardly, but the only thing you can accomplish that way is creative failure.

The thing about shooting, you see, is that if you're serious about it, it tends to be an all-absorbing kind of sport. It's like you're a computer and it's filling up all your memory, it's eating up all your thinking time. And after a while, shooting becomes the only thing that's interesting. Your career isn't really interesting anymore.

In my case, I also have the problem that I'm a writer, and these are grim times for writers. The basic dynamics of the marketplace have changed since I got into it, and all the things which made it an interesting career just don't exist anymore. Now, it's like, "You want another article on some celebrity nitwit? That's fine . . ."

I have a sideline writing for the gun magazines these days, though, and that's fun. It started out as a joke between my friend Mac and me; we decided that we'd write for the gun magazines, because that way we'd get free guns. It seemed like a real good idea at the time. I can sell stories just fine, so I went to it, and now I'm "a gun writer."

At this point, if I could get away with writing just outdoor stuff, that's what I'd do—but the money's just not there. It's two hundred dollars or three hundred dollars an article, tops, so even if you write like crazy you can't do it. I never have gotten a free gun, either: the whole plan was a bust. My shooting's improving, though.

36

"I've found out through shooting that there's more to life than work."

MARY ELLEN MOORE *lives with Michael Bane (previous interview), and is also a writer by profession. She lived around Michael's guns for ten years before taking up shooting herself.*

As Michael said, he was involved in IPSC shooting very haphazardly at first, and that was really irritating to me. He was always last, and he'd come home and grumble. He started thinking about quitting completely, but he really liked the people he shot with and he really looked forward to the matches; it was only after he came home that he was miserable. We talked about it, and he told me that if I were doing it with him, he could really get into it and enjoy it more.

I went to one of the matches, then, and once I got over the hump of meeting the people—basically, I'm not very outgoing—I started to like it. For a long time I'd been a fan of the woman character Purdy on "The New Avengers" TV show. On every show they somehow managed to fit in a sequence in one of those combat "fun houses," with Purdy going through the course in these weird long dresses and high boots, shooting "A" hits on everything, then blowing the smoke from her gun and putting it back on her hip. When I saw that first IPSC match, I thought, "That's just what Purdy does!"

I edged into it gradually, and now I'm really serious about shooting. In fact, shooting is the main reason I'm looking for a job right now; when you're a freelance writer, your time is never really your own, but with a well-defined, permanent job, I can have my own hours when I'm not working. And with a regular paycheck coming in, I can help pay for bullets and new guns and matches and so on. I used to work all the time—all I did was work—but now, even though this sounds trite, I've found out through shooting that there's more to life than work. I'll do my job really well, but I really don't want work to take over my life again, because I'd rather shoot than work.

I think that shooting has helped my self-confidence tremendously. Whenever I used to have to do something hard, I'd think back to when I had to appear on television to promote one of my books, and think, "If I could be on television without passing out, I can do this." Now, I think about shooting: "If I can get up in front of forty people every Sunday and humiliate myself in this strange sport, and come out of it still liking it, I can certainly go interview some housing developer somewhere."

Also, if I put the time into it, I can really see myself doing well at this sport on a national level. The top national IPSC woman shooter has only been doing it three years, she's in no better or worse shape than I am, and she had no more of an edge than me when she started. That's kind of exciting for somebody like me, who's never participated in sports in her life. Maybe, if I'm willing to work at it, I could be the top woman in the field.

"Most shooting activity takes place in the right brain."

DON NYGORD *is an international champion pistol shooter who specializes in air guns. He is pictured in the workroom of his Southern California home with the air pistol with which he won a Gold Medal in the 1981 World Championships.*

The hardest part of this sport is the psychological aspect. In shooting, when you hit the elite level, ninety-five per cent of the problem is psychological. Part of the reason why I did well in the World Championships was that I was psychologically convinced that the gun I had was a unique system, and how could it possibly fail me?

Psychologists have been working at various levels in the area of goal achievement and mental conditioning of the subconscious. That kind of training is probably more important than anything else. We feel that that's probably where the Eastern Bloc people have done their best work. Their equipment is somewhat crude, yet they still perform marvels with it. Their training is very sophisticated—which makes it an extra pleasure when someone like a myopic forty-five-year-old American pops up and manages to beat them for once.

There's the perceptual aspect of seeing, and then of course there's the optical aspect of seeing. In the books the optometrists say that you can't see any finer than a quarter of a diopter, but shooters are trained observers, and I can spot an eighth of a diopter. It's just years of watching for very small differences.

Now we're into the split-brain theory: right brain and left brain. Most shooting activity takes place in the right brain, and I've had some *really* funny experiences myself and heard some strange things. There's a fellow who's a really erratic shooter, especially in the four-second phase of the rapid-fire event; he either hits them all or misses them all. So he was describing how it was when he hit them all, and it was really eerie. He said that he saw the first target, he saw the bullet coming out of the muzzle, the smoke coming out of the gun, the cartridge case blowing off to the side, and simultaneously he saw the fifth target and the bullet coming out of the gun on that target, as well as all the targets in between. He swears to God that he saw this.

I remembered this when I started reading about right brain/left brain activity. The right brain has no time sense. It approaches things in an omnidirectional fashion; it doesn't care where it starts from—the top, the sides, the bottom. There is none of this left-to-right or right-to-left business. So I went back to the guy with this and had him tell me the scene again exactly. What he was describing was pure right brain activity. He saw everything simultaneously.

When I was really shooting well, the year I won the World Championships, I was getting to the point where I would almost always shoot all ten shots inside the ten ring in a three-quarters-of-an-inch group. I'd fire one round at oh, say ten o'clock, and then I'd say, "Well, I think I'm going to fire another one over here at one o'clock just to make a pair of eyes," and POW! there would be a hole at one o'clock. Then I'd go to the center for a nose, then down for three in a row to make a mouth.

I'd start to laugh and think this was just crazy, you know? I can't hold that well, and the gun can't shoot that well. I'd be looking around like, "This is weird. You can't do that. Nobody can do that!"

"I waited for his two beady eyes to come out."

Tony Carlotto *is co-owner of a photography store in Great Barrington, Massachusetts. He also raises horses, pigs, and chickens.*

Hard to say why I first started buying guns. I like western history and that stuff, so I started by buying the replicas.

Had a friend who was a dealer, and he had a few. I saw how they looked; they looked pretty nice. That's how I saw the .44-40. It's an 1875 Remington replica, and I got that. Then I saw the .357, and *it* looked pretty nice. Now I've got about twelve or so.

I use them for playing. Go outside some days and blow up five hundred rounds. Shoot beer cans, pails, raccoons. Usually with coons it's three o'clock in the morning and the neighbors are wondering what's going on. Last coon was a big one, in the barn. I'd just got a new gun, that little Bernardelli. Never fired it till then. I went up to the barn and the coon got out the window. Come back, and I was laying in bed and I hear the chickens going crazy, so I went back out and he's eating all the eggs and he's got a couple of them inside there, so I waited for his two beady eyes to come out, and let loose with it. Worked pretty good.

At first I didn't have the heart to shoot coons, but after they started destroying everything—probably cost me two or three hundred bucks' worth of feed and vitamins and that—I started getting mad. Then this last one shit on my power saw, and I said, "That's it, there's no more heart for *them.*"

My favorite gun is that 1863 Springfield rifle there, black powder. That's a lot of fun. I bought it one day, took it out and fired it, and at a hundred yards I missed the bull's-eye by two inches, first time I fired it. Then I did it twice more, so I got to like that idea. Plus it's inexpensive to shoot, plus the history involved in it. There's Civil War history in it, western history in it.

I like the .357 too. Use it for plinking around. Expensive way to do it, though—twenty bucks for fifty shells.

Plinking's great. My cousin comes over and he's got a .22 pump just like that Winchester I got, so I'll let him shoot a lot of my rounds. Chicken eggs once in a while from the porch. I got one on the first shot once; figured that wasn't too smart. We figured it'd take us about 25 rounds, and I got it first shot. Just to make it exciting one day I took a *Playboy* centerfold and shot the tits out of it with two shots, right through the nipples from a hundred feet with that 'scope on it.

I've never been in trouble with guns. I got shot in the ass with a pellet gun once when I was a kid, but that's about it. We used to have wars with BB guns, wore winter coats in summertime and the pellets would bounce off, but this one kid had a pellet gun he could cock up about twenty times so it was real powerful, and he got me in the left cheek. I only found it about two months ago, 'cause it was starting to come out. Well, actually, it was my wife who found it.

"It's one of the last freedoms we have in this country."

KURT HERRMANN, *a New York advertising executive, lives in Connecticut. One of the guns he owns is a one-hundred-seventy-five-dollar mail-order replica of a .45 Thompson ("Tommy") gun. Federally designated a "non-gun," the Thompson will not fire.*

Anything that's unique appeals to me, or something that nobody else has. How many people around here would have Thompsons? I'd say there weren't any. I feel this makes me unique, like the car that I drive, the clothes that I wear, the audio equipment that I buy and use—everything. I feel that I'm an individualist.

I throw parties here every year, and we were going to have a 1920s speakeasy party with the clothes and the records and everything, and I thought that definitely I had to get a machine gun. I was calling on an agency, and the gal had to excuse herself. She had the Sharper Image catalogue on her desk, and I was flipping through it while I was waiting, and there it was, the Thompson! So I grabbed the phone and I called and ordered it on my Visa card, and by the time she came back and said "What are you doing?" I just said "I just called and ordered a machine gun." Haa! That's how it all started.

I always wanted to get one of these, because I like the historical conversational value it has. It's not something you normally see in somebody's living room when you go over to their house.

The first reaction is, "Is it real?"

I sort of go along with it. I say, "Of course it is. Why?"

They say, "Isn't it illegal?"

"Not in Connecticut."

"Oh, really? Does it fire?"

"Yeah. I take it to the range once in a while with some friends and we all fire it."

Eventually I let them in on the fact that it's only a replica and I have it just because it played a big part in our country's history in the twenties.

I think that was an interesting period. It was a very tragic period. I'm not supporting that period, but I think the costumes that they wore, and everything else, were very interesting, like other periods in our country and the world. The killings and the murders that went on were very tragic not only to the people who were involved—their own little group, "The Mob" as they called it—but also to the innocent people that got in the way accidentally.

Sometimes I pick the Thompson up and look mean and pull out one of the records from the era and imagine what it was like.

I would have been a federal man. In fact, when I was looking at careers I was considering the FBI. That changed because my father was a major influence on me getting into advertising, but I was very serious about joining the FBI.

I'm an NRA member because I think it's one of the last freedoms we have in this country, and if they take that away from us we have nothing. If the Soviets knew that Americans didn't have guns in their homes, they would find a very easy way to get in here. As long as everybody has a weapon in their home—or at least the Soviets *think* we do—they have no chance over here. That's one of our last freedoms in the strength of our country.

"There was a hole through the wall that was really kinda large."

JACK "COWBOY" CLEMENT *is a Nashville record producer/ songwriter whose clients include Johnny Cash and Waylon Jennings.*

I was in the Marine Corps, you know. Got an "Expert" marksmanship badge, which ain't that easy. I was classified as an MP and was on the drill team, so I had three weapons: a .45 pistol, an M-1 rifle, and an old Springfield '03 with a chrome-plated bayonet.

The Springfield was better balanced for drilling than the M-1, see. You could flip it in the air with the bayonet on. I perfected what I called "the double toss": the rifle would flip twice, then come down with the bayonet sticking in the ground. That would bend the bayonet, of course, but you could bend it back. When they chrome-plated them, that took the temper out of them, see. I had a lot of fun on the drill team.

The .30-30 I have now is a nice gun, but I don't shoot it much. The elevator on the sights is missing, for one thing. I found that out one night when I decided it was time to try it out. I'd had it a year or two, and I had a few rounds, and I thought it would be perfectly safe to squeeze off a few rounds here in the house if I got me a proper backdrop.

I looked over at the door. It was an unnecessary door, and I hadn't gotten around to tearing it out, so I decided to write myself a little note to remind myself about that by blowing the shit out of the doorknob.

I went and got my gun and loaded it up. I squeezed off a round into the floor just to make sure it was working, then got away from the door a bit, lined it up real good, and squeezed it off. You don't jerk the trigger, you know—you *squeeeeeeze* the trigger. You got to line 'em up and *squeeeeeeze* 'em off.

I fully expected to see that doorknob just disintegrate before my eyes, but it didn't, so I thought, "Well, I'll take a little better aim." I lined it up again and squeezed off another one, but still nothing happened.

I decided to go down and take a look. I saw that my grouping was pretty good; it was just low. Then I looked at the gun, and sure enough, the little elevator on the sights wasn't there. No wonder I was shooting low!

I went back to the door, and oho, I'd done shot through it. I went looking for holes. There were holes out the back of the door—those were a little bigger than the holes in the front—and then there was a hole through a wall that was really kinda large. Then I noticed that the radio on the receptionist's desk was shattered, and beyond that there was a hole through the front window, going out toward houses where a bunch of kids were sleeping and stuff. Ooooooooooh . . .

Anyway, I decided "No more squeezing off rounds in the house." I've still got a nice little .22 around here, though, and I can hit some things with that.

"When you play the game, you leave the adult world behind you."

JERRY BRAUN *(right) runs a New York-area Survival Games dealership with offices in Mount Kisco, New York. The game is played by teams armed with paint-pellet CO_2 guns, the object being to capture the opposing team's flag.*

The game started with a discussion between a stockbroker from the city and a novelist from the country about who was better able to survive in a primitive environment —a city person who is more adept and aware of dangers present or lurking, or somebody who is more accustomed to a primitive environment and able to adapt to it. They saw the pistol, which is used to mark cattle and trees and the like, in a farm magazine, and they invented the Survival Game around it. The game caught on, and now it's expanding very fast: my operation has tripled in size within a year.

The people who come to play it are all sorts, from the presidents of major corporations to people who work in a warehouse. Mostly they live in cities. We get a lot of Wall Street people, for instance.

The game is not about killing. It is, rather, a hunt-and-chase game, and it is primal. Children play hunt-and-chase games, like tag and hide-and-seek, in every culture, but they have to be conditioned and taught how to associate the hunt with the kill. In our game, there is no kill: people who are shot with the paint pellet are not harmed. There is no feeling of real physical peril, and there is no aggression or hostility between players during the game or when the game is over. The players go back to a childhood state during the game, and the game is a release: you have more chance of getting into a fight seeing a movie than you do playing the game. When you play the game, you leave your adult world behind you.

And the game is a great leveler: we have military people playing against accountants, and people who fought the war in Vietnam playing side by side with people who protested it.

On that point, I don't think the game could have flourished in the sixties—but I don't think the movie *Star Wars* could have happened in the sixties, either. The sixties was an era not of imagination, but of confrontation and introspective social consciousness, an era of a crusade. I don't think that people would have given the game a chance in the sixties. Now they do, and they enjoy it. Over 50 percent of the people who play the game come back to play again.

The game can even be positively therapeutic. One of the people who played in the first World Championships had nightmares of his experiences in Vietnam, but when he played the game his nightmares dissipated and eventually went away. Other people may feel differently, of course: we've had two guys come up after the game and say, "This really isn't for me. It brings back memories I'd rather not have"—but that's only happened twice among tens of thousands of players.

The very first game was won by a forester without firing a shot, and the first person eliminated from the game was a venture capitalist from New York City—but in subsequent games, the city people acquitted themselves well. The original question has never been resolved, then, but that never was the main point: the main point is fun.

"Fokker knew that it would work, but the bigwigs wouldn't believe him."

COLE PALEN, *pictured with his flare gun beneath the muzzles of the twin Spandau machine guns on his World War I Fokker Triplane, is the proprietor of the famous vintage-aircraft flying circus in Rhinebeck, New York.*

In the beginning, when a Frenchman and a German met in the sky, their paths were just crossing as they flew over each other's territory, trying to find out what was going on. They would wave to each other, because they were sharing the excitement and beauty of flying. They were well fed, and they wore the best uniforms and flew the best planes, and that was the way to fight a war: just wave at your enemy.

The fighting started one day when one pilot, instead of waving, thumbed his nose at the other guy. The next time they met, there was a pistol; then there was a rifle, then a machine gun firing out to the side of the airplane, then a machine gun fixed to the top wing and firing over the propeller.

Some of those early rigs were something else. On the British FE-2B, for instance, which was a "pusher" plane, the gunner had to use one gun for shooting ahead, then climb up over the pilot to another gun mounted on top of a ladder whenever they were attacked from behind, then climb back to his seat.

Then along came a poor daredevil stunt pilot flying for the military, one Roland Garros, who realized that if he could fire the machine gun straight down the line of flight of the airplane, he wouldn't have to fly in one direction and shoot in another: he could just aim the whole airplane. He thought about it, and came up with a way to do it. He mounted the gun behind the whirling blades of the propeller, to the back of which he had attached triangular steel plates, and fired: some bullets flew out between the blades, and the ones that hit the blades simply bounced off.

For a few weeks, Garros was the terror of the skies—but firing the gun into the propeller blades was like hitting them with a sledgehammer, though, so finally his propeller broke, and he had to glide down and land in a meadow. And since the hunting had been so much better over German-held territory than over French, all the people who ran up to his plane were speaking German.

When the Germans realized they had captured Roland Garros, the Terror of the Skies, they sent all their best technicians to inspect his plane and find out how he did this marvelous thing. One of those Germans was Anthony Fokker, one of their leading aircraft designers. He laughed when he saw the little plates on the blades, and within forty-eight hours came up with a mechanical means of linking the engine to the machine gun. All the parts within an engine are connected to other parts with gears or connecting rods or cams or push rods or whatever, and everything is precisely timed, and Fokker just extended this back to the machine gun: when a little cam connected to the engine came up and said "Don't shoot," because the propeller was in the way, the gun didn't shoot.

Fokker knew that it would work—it was so ridiculously simple—but the bigwigs wouldn't believe him. Even though he was a civilian, they made him go up in a plane and prove the synchronization gear worked by shooting down an enemy plane. Fokker went up, but he couldn't do it, so they got their ace, Max Immelman, to try it. It worked fine, and the Germans ruled the skies until the Allies found out how the synchronization gear worked. Then the dogfights *really* got started.

"It's better than anything the Russians have."

CAPTAIN TONY PARKER *is a flight instructor on the F-16, the United States Air Force's frontline combat fighter aircraft. He is pictured at MacDill AFB, Florida, as armorers load 20-millimeter cannon ammunition into his fighter.*

Basically, a fighter aircraft is a flying gun, and that hasn't changed much. The F-16 is a flying weapons system configured for air-to-air and air-to-ground combat with a variety of weapons, but for close-in fighting and strafing it relies on its gun.

That's something we learned in Vietnam. Initially, our F-4 fighters did not carry an internal gun. Unless they were carrying a gun pod, they had bad problems with MIGs that got inside the range of their missiles. Now, all U.S. fighter aircraft are produced with an internal gun.

The gun itself is an old weapon—it's the same six-barreled 20-millimeter cannon that's been in service since the late 1950s—but it does the job. Its maximum rate of fire is six thousand rounds a minute, and you really don't need more than that. That's a hundred rounds a second which can be put into a very small piece of sky, and one 20-millimeter round in the right place will have a very negative effect on any airframe. The F-16 carries enough ammunition for about five very short bursts.

The gun is very reliable; it's a proven weapon, and in combination with the F-16's computer sighting system it's pretty definitive. The computer is the key to it; it cuts out a lot of guesswork and reduces the margin of error substantially. With this system, once the sight is punched up in visual display and the radar is locked in on the target, the computer makes a lot of calculations that previously had to be made by the pilot. For instance, it calculates the range of the target, the G's the target is pulling, the G's your own aircraft is pulling, and the gravity drop of the rounds once they're fired.

Basically, the computer makes sure that the rounds actually arrive exactly where you aim them—right on the target in a tracking shot, ahead of him in most other shots—by compensating for the various motion factors working against that result.

The computer does that very well, too. Vietnam-era computer gunsights had to make assumptions about movement which were not necessarily true, but this is new technology, and when the radar is locked onto the target, it doesn't make assumptions. Instead, it instantly collates observed data on what's actually happening, so that what you see is what you get. It works very well indeed, even without a radar lock.

This whole weapons system, in fact, is really great. It's the best there is. This is it, right here: this aircraft is the most sophisticated, most maneuverable fighter in the sky. It's the premier fighter of the Free World, and it's better than anything the Russians have.

That feels good, of course, but really, air-to-air combat hasn't changed that much. The other guy can still make unexpected moves, and he might survive your hits and come back at you, or his wingman might be working on you at the same time—all those factors are still operating in any dogfight. American technology gives us an edge, but it's not a guarantee by any means.

No, it's still hairy, even with the F-16. The pilot still has to make an awful lot of fast, correct decisions under a lot of pressure. That's why fighter pilots have to be such aggressive, competitive people. When it comes down to it, the guy who gets the other guy in his sights is still the winner.

"I am the last of the Zacchinis."

HUGO ZACCHINI *is a professional "human cannonball." He is pictured in his Tampa, Florida, machine shop with his cannon, which was built there by his father, the great Edmond Zacchini.*

The cannon act is spectacular, but it also has to be beautiful. You have to know how to launch out of that thing, and once in the air you have to be in a nice, arched position, similar to a swan dive but with your arms out in front of you—a naturally beautiful position—and then you have to execute a slow three-quarters turn so that you land neatly on your back in the net. That takes balance, reflexes, and the orientation capability a person has between the ears which tells him when he is out of position, coordinated with what the eyes see. The position in the air is crucial: if the projectile has to scramble and barely makes a safe landing, it's still a man shot from a cannon, but it's not beautiful.

The accident rate is not as great as you might expect when people are shot from cannons at up to 90 m.p.h., because projectiles are picked for their natural balancing and athletic talent, then trained gradually, beginning with short jumps. The most dangerous part is the landing: I've had the net collapse under me a half-dozen times, but usually it breaks your fall even if it collapses, and I've only been seriously hurt once.

The design of the cannon is a family secret; I am still doing the act, so we refrain from talking about it. Our design is the most successful, though, and the one that others try to copy. The cannon I use was built by my father in 1946 on a Diamond T chassis. I have another of his cannons which I don't use: that one's the double, which

shoots two people a fraction of a second apart, and it still has the photographic darkroom my father built in it; photography was his hobby. The double act is beautiful—but it takes three trained people to operate, and I have only one trained assistant.

That double act took an awful lot of confidence to do day after day on something like a Ringling route. They'd have to move all the equipment every day—all the wires and cables and everything—and set it up again for two people firing in succession and landing in the same net without colliding. Doing something like that takes an awful lot of courage, and that my father had.

I would not be in this business if it hadn't been for my father, a dedicated family man and a mechanical genius. Although crippled by a trapeze accident, he fired all his brothers from the cannon, and he outlasted all of them. He kept touring with the cannon until he was over eighty years of age: he was the first to start and the last to go, and he was Mr. Cannon.

The most spectacular record was achieved by my uncle Emmanuel, who was fired over three ferris wheels placed side by side. That was the most sensational thing which ever happened in the carnival business. For myself, I hope to indisputably hold the record for the number of years with the act, and the number of performances. I am still relatively young, but I am the last of the Zacchinis in the business. The others gave it up, retired to better or less worrisome businesses, and no kind words or moments of high blood pressure from me were able to change that. Nobody goes over Niagara Falls in a barrel because somebody else wants them to.

"It's an American heritage you're looking at here."

GARY HERMAN *trades in fine guns from his Connecticut store. He is pictured there with a set of American guns considered to be the world's finest contemporary example of gun craft and engraving.*

Lynton McKenzie, an English engraver, created this set to commemorate his becoming a citizen of the United States in 1976. It is the most elaborate contemporary set known to exist today; the workmanship is incomparably above anything I have seen in twenty years of looking at the best, with the possible exception of some Nicholas Bouté work from France way back when.

Its motif is pure Americana. The rifle is an 1873 Winchester in .44-40, and the revolver is its companion piece, the Colt Frontier Model also in .44-40—in the frontier days a man would carry these guns because he could use the same ammunition in both of them—while the derringer and the Bowie knife complete the set of classic American weapons. It's an American heritage you're looking at here, and that's what Lynton had in mind: he wanted to show everybody how happy he was about becoming a citizen, and celebrate the history of this country in the best way he knew. That's a nice motivation, and the result is simply magnificent.

The ivory work alone took him over two and a half years, and the detail work extends even to the engraving of the hinges on the seasoned mahogany case and the hand turning of all the bottles which are part of the kit, all of which he did himself; he even left the guns in the white—in their naked-steel condition, without plating or case coloring—so that you could see that there were no imperfections, which

of course there aren't. The Bowie knife, a collaboration between Lynton and D. E. Henry, is optically perfect; when you hold it up to the light, you see no ripples, no waves—nothing—in the blade.

The set really does it all. It is close to perfection in mechanics, workmanship, engraving, art, engineering, woodwork, fit, finish—all the elements that combine in high-grade guns. If you're interested in any or all of those elements, you really have to be interested in high-grade guns; some of the finest work in each field is to be found in them.

Through history, fine guns have been appreciated and seen as an important part of their heritage by all the kings and queens and great families, and at present that kind of appreciation is returning quite strongly as a popular phenomenon. We have been through a cycle of plebeian interest in firepower, full-automatic laser-sighted technology and so on, but now the cycle is reversing and different values are becoming more desirable on the marketplace. The highest sales by the fine Italian high-grade gun manufacturers right now, for instance, are of old-style hammer guns, while in this country there are now hunting seasons for shooters of traditional black-powder and muzzle-loader guns. The high-tech guns made hunting too easy, you see, so now people are becoming more and more interested in guns that are more sporting, that which represent more of a challenge to the shooter.

Along with this trend goes a rising level of appreciation for the values of skill and craftsmanship and art over pure technology, and that of course is to be welcomed.

"My gun had become a topic of conversation all over the world."

BIJAN, *the internationally famous men's clothing designer, achieved some notoriety in the fashion world with his line of bullet-resistant clothing and his ten thousand-dollar gold-plated .38 Special Colt revolver. He is pictured in the office of his Rodeo Drive, Beverly Hills, boutique.*

Personally, I do not like guns. Personally, I am more in silk and double-breasted and single-breasted suits and wool and cashmere and those things. But that has no meaning. If you do anything in good taste, the market is there for it.

I am a designer. I design for men all over the world; they are kings, presidents, senators, doctors, attorneys, actors, princes, businessmen. My philosophy as a designer is that I should always bring something different to these men.

Everything I design is a fact of life, something that is already available in the world—but after I put my taste into it, it is very different. And one thing is always in mind: quality. All this could be in a line of men's clothing for fall, or a summer collection, or a tuxedo to be made, a chinchilla bedspread, a perfume for men in Baccarat bottles, a gun.

To the average person, what I do is a little bit crazy, a little bit outrageous, and quite controversial, but my clients understand the quality. And being a men's designer includes being an artist—an artist in taste, and an artist in knowing what is going on in the world—and so I know that nowadays, anybody who is very famous or very rich is a target. Believe me! Protection is something very important to them. So I took this bullet-resistant material, Kevlar, which is very light and thin, and I designed it into my lines of clothing between the fabric and the lining. Then the man is protected, and he looks wonderful because he is wearing a Bijan suit, so he feels good. I decided not to charge my clients for such clothing if they wanted it.

Then on one of the trips I made to visit a client—he is head of a country in Europe; you know him—he asked me to do something that was masculine and different and chic, something that as a gift would be most impressive. I want to swim against the river, so I thought that if I designed a gun, it would be different; it would be something that maybe a lot of people would not like, but it would be controversial, and it would be chic and pretty and well worth the money.

So I had the opportunity to make and sell a limited edition of two hundred guns, all numbered. I made the grip of dark blue leather in my factory in Italy. My organization in conjunction with Colt produced the gun. We used seventeen or eighteen layers of blue ink polish in the custom shop to make it that particular dark, beautiful blue. We used fifty-six grams of gold to make that simple but very pretty finish on the cylinder and the other parts. We used a special mink for the cover, placed it in a beautiful beveled Lucite box, and then enclosed it in a black velvet bag. The reason for the box was to do something so that people would not carry the gun. It would be something that people would keep in their home and discuss.

I was so proud and happy to hear that my gun had become a topic of conversation all over the world. The most beautiful recognition I got was from a particular royal family in Europe who told me that. Forgive me please for saying this, but many royal families and personalities bought the gun to say, "Thank you, Bijan."

"American guns started to go bad after World War II."

ANDY MORANDI, *eighty-one, has spent his whole life collect-ing and trading guns of all sorts. Formerly a restaurateur and hotelier, he now runs a small cheese- and ham-smoking business near Hillsdale, New York.*

The good guns are a great investment, but you have to know what you're doing.

For instance, there's that .22 Hornet up there on the wall, that Brno made in Czechoslovakia that I paid a hun-dred-and-some dollars for thirty years ago. A year ago I checked in some catalogs, and the gun in "good used" con-dition was up to $750 or $780.

That's because there isn't a good .22 Hornet made in America. There's a couple of small American companies making a .22 Hornet now, but we gun people term them as being made out of "plowshare" material. Terrible. That Brno is the smoothest darn thing you ever saw. Of course, they don't make them any more.

Winchesters were a good investment—until Winchester started to go bad. Anybody buying Winchesters likes to have them made before World War II or before 1964. Since '64 they started to go bad. They've come out with those Replica models and Commemorative models, and they've gone over pretty well, but old-timers like me turn down our noses. We know there's a dollar in 'em, but we don't want these replicas. You want the genuine stuff, whether it's honey or salad dressing or butter. If you want butter, you want butter. You want cheese, you want *cheese.*

They're making an artificial cheese now, y'know. Kraft has it.

American guns started to go bad after World War II. German guns, too. Before then, there used to be a lot of handwork done on those guns. When they assembled them, they did it by hand—this one needed to be ground down a little bit here, that one needed to be ground down a little bit there—but then World War II came along and the factories all turned to making war materials and run-ning twenty-four hours a day and pushing the stuff out. That gave the gun manufacturers the idea, so they started mass production, and the quality of our guns started to go bad.

Jap guns used to be terrible, but those Japs got smart. And I'll tell you, you take a look at these bums who don't want to work, that work in *our* factories—that are pushed by the unions and talked into saying they're worth so much money an hour to sit around and suck cigarettes and spend half their time in the restroom and not show up on Mon-days—and you'll see why we gun people a few years ago said "We'd better sit up and pay attention to some of these Jap guns!"

You have to watch Spanish guns, too. Spain years ago made poor guns, but *they've* learned how to make good guns. The Aya is a good gun, for instance, and I've got a .22 automatic pistol that I bought a year ago just for plinking, and if that isn't the sweetest thing! And it's made in *Spain!*

60

"We're not hassled so much these days by the liberal anti-gun media."

BOB MAGEE, *pictured with an Austrian AUG-SA rifle, is an executive of Interarms, the largest American importer of commercial firearms and the largest privately owned gun company in the world.*

Interarms is in a good position these days because we deal in high-quality imports. I think it is fair to say that the overall quality of American firearms, with a few notable exceptions such as Ruger, is going down, while the quality of many foreign guns is improving, and that helps our business.

European arms designers and manufacturers seem to have a definite edge right now because they're developing new concepts and looking at new methods and materials. Designing and marketing a gun is a very expensive and risky business, and the Europeans seem willing to take those chances. Costs in the American gun industry have risen tremendously, so most U.S. companies are following the design lead shown by the Europeans, particularly the Germans and Austrians; their technology has always been hard to beat, and it still is.

The British have always been known for very fine hand-tooled guns, but that's becoming a thing of the past. Few young gunmakers seem willing to spend all those years learning the craft, and not too many sportsmen are willing to buy hunting rifles costing several thousand dollars. The Japanese are making a lot of guns now, and another source to watch for all kinds of guns is China: right now, Chinese guns are crude by our standards, but it won't take them long to learn what appeals to American sportsmen.

There are a lot of interesting new imports coming through Interarms, so my job stays pretty fascinating. I must admit, though, that it's not quite as much fun as it used to be. The 1968 Gun Control Act (GCA), which was aimed to a considerable degree at Interarms, put an end to military surplus firearms and all the business they helped

generate. Interarms was founded as the Korean conflict wound down, and until the '68 GCA we dealt mostly in mail-order military surplus. And surplus was great for the industry. For about thirty-five dollars, you could order a Springfield or a Mauser—a really high-quality firearm—and that kind of bargain got a lot of people into the shooting sports who otherwise couldn't have afforded that first step. Along with the surplus boom came small dealers, custom stock-makers and gunsmiths to work on those guns. That was a whole peripheral industry, and the whole thing just died after 1968. It was a very sad time for everybody in the business—everybody, that is, except some of the big U.S. gun companies who quietly supported the GCA because they saw surplus arms as a threat to their business.

But back in the surplus days, it was great. When you were opening a crate, you never knew exactly what you'd find in it. There was some really exotic stuff—original Henry rifles mixed in with a bunch of Winchesters, a Volcanic pistol, all kinds of unusual Lugers, everything you can imagine—and it was really exciting. Those really were the good old days.

On the other hand, we're not hassled so much these days by the liberal anti-gun media since the '68 GCA ended direct mail order and military surplus. There was a time, after the assassination of President Kennedy, when over-zealous newspaper/TV types would write in attempting to order guns using the name Lee Harvey Oswald or Hydell, the alias he used when he ordered the Carcano rifle used in Dallas from a company in Chicago. What they were attempting was, in most cases, highly illegal, but they conveniently overlooked that in trying to make a case against the gun industry.

These days those people only come around when things get slack and they need to fill some space. Gun dealers always seem to make an easy mark for the media.

"Conglomerate owners ran gun companies into the ground."

BILL RUGER, JR., *followed his father into the gun-manufacturing business. He is pictured on the shop floor of the Sturm, Ruger & Company plant in Southport, Connecticut.*

My education was in electronic engineering, and I worked in that field for several years, then came to work for the company by my own choice. It was not one of those situations in which the son is forced to follow in the father's footsteps. Like any other business, of course, this one has its daily frustrations, but I have been around gun people all my life, and have many strong attachments to people in the gun world. The development and successful introduction of a new product gives satisfaction, and while growth has been slow over the years, it has been steady, and one can look back on it with a certain amount of pride.

I would say that in the commercial market, the overall quality of American guns is improving. It is true that these days there are fewer manufacturers and fewer different models of gun being manufactured than there were in the fifties and sixties, but the models still available are if anything better made and better designed than they were during that expansion period.

The "shake-out" or disappearance of some manufacturers occurred during the expansion period prior to 1980, when gun sales leveled off and began to decline somewhat. I would have to ascribe it to internal mismanagement of some sort, suffered largely at the hands of conglomerate owners, rather than to a lack of quality products or the vicissitudes of the marketplace. Conglomerate owners in many cases ran gun companies into the ground, and while many manufacturers eventually became independent of their conglomerate owners, very often it was too late.

At this point in time, American firearms manufacturers are either independent companies or, like Colt and Smith & Wesson, divisions of conglomerates which pretty much leave them alone to conduct their business. Overall (though not necessarily), it seems that gun manufacturing companies tend to do better when they are run by "gun people."

Sturm, Ruger is of course an independent company with family management and majority family ownership, and we do well in the commercial market. We have introduced several successful new models in recent years, and on the whole we are certainly holding our own with other domestic manufacturers and foreign companies.

In terms of new designs, we and most other American manufacturers concentrate on relatively inexpensive hunting and working firearms—for example, this company's 10/.22 and Mini-14 semi-automatic models, which are ideal for the person who wants a reliable, relatively inexpensive, relatively high-quality gun suitable to a number of tasks—while European manufacturers, whose domestic markets are limited to the military, the police, and the relatively affluent sport shooter, concentrate on assault rifles, semi-automatic pistols, and expensive sporting guns. We introduce more new models and create design innovations in our field, while the Europeans have the lead in theirs.

"The machine guns legally licensed to collectors are almost never involved in crimes."

BILL DOUGLAS *has been collecting U.S. and other military guns since he was six years old. Professionally, he runs an insurance business in Dunedin, Florida.*

I have about fifty-five automatic weapons now. I've always enjoyed studying history, particularly the military and police history of the United States and the part that weapons played in it. You buy a gun, and you get a book to find out more about it, and it goes on from there.

There's all that, and then there's the design and engineering of the weapon, all the different techniques and developments. You try to put yourself in the shoes of somebody like John Browning, who was one of the most prolific gun inventors, and you try to figure out how he developed these weapons.

The "potato digger" that I have was one of his guns, and it was the first gas-operated machine gun adopted by the U.S. It came about while he was watching some rifles being fired out behind his shop. There were some reeds nearby, and every time the rifles fired, the blast from the muzzles would bend those reeds back. That's when John Browning realized how powerful that muzzle blast was, and started figuring out how it could be used to operate an automatic weapon. That was one of those moments which changed world history, and I have one of the guns that came from it.

So it's an absorbing hobby, and I have to be careful not to give it a disproportionate amount of time. I spend a couple of nights a week talking to other collectors and reading all the literature, and I go to the shows about once a month, and I give my little talks and lectures; it's a relaxing way to spend time and get away from the frustrations of being an insurance agent.

It's not as much fun as it used to be, though, because the value of U.S. military guns, and particularly automatic weapons, is escalating rather drastically. In 1968, you see, the government decided that there were too many unlicensed machine guns out there, and granted a one-month amnesty. If you had an automatic weapon, you could bring it in either to surrender it or get it licensed—but after that, there was no way to license such a gun. Today, if you find a German machine gun your uncle brought back from World War II, there is no way to own it legally. You have to turn it in for destruction or be liable for prosecution.

What that means, of course, is that the pool of machine guns that can be owned and traded legally is frozen, so the value has gone out of sight. I used to trade a lot, but now it's kind of like trading two twenty-five-thousand-dollar cats for a fifty-thousand-dollar dog. A lot of doctors and lawyers are getting into collecting machine guns now; it takes that kind of income.

Personally, I am anticipating that my collection will be an aid in my retirement planning. On the other hand, automatic weapons are getting a lot of negative publicity from the so-called "cocaine cowboys" with their MAC-10s down in Miami, and it may be just a matter of time before somebody says that they shouldn't be privately owned anymore.

That's something we all think about a lot. The machine guns legally licensed to collectors are almost never involved in crimes; the "cocaine cowboys" are using automatic weapons bought illegally and never registered, or they are buying semi-automatic assault rifles and then illegally converting them into machine guns. Unfortunately, the press doesn't usually make such fine distinctions, and legal machine gun owners end up lumped in with the bad guys.

KNOW YOUR ENEMY

"That's the attraction: smoothly functioning machinery, and the acquisition of power."

CHRISTOPHER WRIGHT *is a freelance writer/photographer and a recently initiated gun owner. She is pictured sharpening her Florida dove-hunting skills in New England's Berkshire Hills.*

I like guns because they're very solid, precise, well-made instruments. They make great noises: when you work the action of a gun, it makes a nice, satisfying click, and you know that this instrument is going to do what you want it to do.

I remember that from my first experience with guns, which was target shooting at summer camp with bolt-action .22 rifles. I liked the sound and the feel of working the bolt action as much as I liked seeing the little holes appear in the target.

After I quit going to summer camp, I didn't have much to do with guns until my former husband's brother took me dove hunting. I found that I liked that as much as I had liked shooting when I was a little girl, and for somebody who hadn't picked up a gun in years, I did okay: I brought down half-a-dozen doves my first time out, and I thought that was just terrific.

I wasn't squeamish about it. In fact, I was the opposite. I liked the whole experience. I had been a fisherperson for years, and as a child I was an avid dissector of small animals, so I guess I never have been a squeamish person. I didn't even mind picking up the doves and snapping their little necks if they were still flopping around, then cleaning them when we got them home. In fact, I adapted a little

Kliban poem about cats and "mousies" to my feelings about dove hunting:

> Love to shoot them dovies
> Watch them hit the ground
> Bite they little heads off
> And blow they feathers 'round.

Since that first dove hunt, which was eight years ago, I have wanted to own a shotgun. Very recently I took care of that wish with a very pretty little Ithica Model 100 12-gauge, side-by-side. I like the notion of having a 12-gauge, not something smaller. It packs a wallop even with the recoil pad I've had put on it, but I know from experience that when you're out in the field and caught up in the excitement of the hunt, you don't notice the recoil. You only notice it the next day, when your shoulder is black-and-blue.

I don't know how much I'll use that shotgun, but I just love owning it. It makes the sweetest of gun sounds when you swing the barrels up to close it. I like the sound my 9-millimeter semi-automatic pistol makes when I chamber a round, too, and that also is a satisfying gun to own.

Another thing I like about guns is the sense of power, and the real power, they give me. With a gun, I have more control over my own destiny—more control over potential events around me, and more personal power. That's the attraction: the satisfaction that comes from smoothly functioning machinery, and the acquisition of power.

68

"I love being isolated, quiet and observant . . ."

DOUGLAS KENYON *owns a Chicago art gallery. He is pictured in Ontario, Canada, with his side-by-side Browning 12-gauge.*

My hunting is associated with our summer home in the Lake of the Woods region of Northwestern Ontario, and, of course, one of the highlights is duck hunting in the fall. When the northern bluebills pass through they're very thick, and it is great sport.

I have a dear friend up there—a local man, Smokey Fadden, and he is the one who acquainted me with every aspect of the area over many years. He has been on that particular body of water for sixty-plus years, and knows everything there is to know about it. His ability to read all those many subtle signs of nature and share them with me has entitled me to a rare, in-depth course in woodmanship that very few people have been able to experience and enjoy. I suppose my infatuation for the kinds of experiences I enjoy up there goes back to my childhood when my father and I would set out on a frosty morning pheasant hunt—a mutual quest between friends with very few words but an extremely close bond.

In addition to duck hunting in Lake of the Woods, I always enjoy a goose hunt in James Bay. It is great to share a pot of coffee and the warmth of a potbellied stove with a few fellow hunters in that predawn darkness. Then we all go our separate ways over the frozen tundra with our Cree Indian guides. Don't ask me how, but somehow the guide gets you to the place where he wants to be, and you settle in to watch the sunrise and thousands of geese move inland, in constant waves, to feed. I love being isolated, quiet and observant, spending time with myself and thinking. It also makes one feel close to the land. If you are sensitive and attuned to what is happening around you, your stalking will lead to a successful hunt. When you ignore the wind direction or where the sun comes up or what the geese feed on, your quest turns into an empty-handed, mindless stroll.

And, of course, it is great to be with friends who enjoy the same things, with the least important thing being who shot what and how many. There are hunters who are concerned with those statistics, but I believe that to be very bad form. Style is very important.

A good gun is a nice companion. One of my favorite guns is my side-by-side Browning 12-gauge. It fits me well, and at times becomes an unconscious extension of me that I have confidence in. Many guns don't seem to have that feel but are instead a contrary piece of hardware. When a hunter is blessed with a good gun that obeys him and a good dog that obeys, life can be quite complete. And nothing is better than fresh duck, wild rice, and a good bottle of wine back at a warm camp with a fire in the fireplace.

The hunt sharpens my senses and is the vehicle for the total experience. I think that I might feel quite silly sitting on a beaver house in the middle of a wild rice bay, waiting for the sun to come up and feeling the utter magnificence of the wild world, if I didn't have a gun in my hand. I don't know that I would do it.

"With grouse, the dog knows and you don't."

RALPH M. PLYMPTON *is a retired financial printing executive and lifetime bird hunter living in Cambridge, New York. He turned ninety in 1984.*

I started to hunt when I was about ten years old in Wellesley, Massachusetts. My grandfather gave me a little single-barreled 12-gauge, and I've been hunting ever since. I got this Browning here for fifty-eight dollars from a gun-dealer feller whose store was going out of business. I can't tell you his name, because that's an eight-hundred or nine-hundred-dollar gun, and if Browning ever found out about it, that feller would never sell another Browning.

I shot grouse mostly when I was young. It wasn't legal to hunt pheasant—or as I call them, "Chinese chickens." As I understand, the English dukes and lords went over to China to exploit the Chinese, and brought these highly privileged Chinese chickens back to put them on their estates: a pheasant egg has got it all over a chicken egg, you know, just like a chicken egg has it all over a duck egg. Massachusetts was the first state to import them into this country around 1900, and the season was closed on them until 1914.

Even when I was in business, I always took the darned time to hunt and fish, and I wasn't a bad shot. I used to hunt chucker partridges with a pistol on a reserve, and I could shoot their heads off in close.

I like to hunt better than I like to fish. You don't need a dog to fish, you see. The dog work is the main part of bird hunting, and that's what I like. I've had dogs all along, except for when I first got married and lived in an apartment.

The first dog I had was a stop hound, which is halfway between a beagle and a foxhound. I'd never heard of them until I bought one. I'd hunt rabbit and fox with it, and it would work on birds too. With a wounded bird, it would follow it, and stop baying; that's why they called it a stop hound. It would put its paws on the bird and hold it until you came up. Since then I've had about ten good dogs, all English pointers. A pointer just likes to hunt; he's not happy just to be around, like a Labrador is. I've had some bum ones, too.

You can't hunt grouse without dogs, see, and I've learned more about grouse hunting from the dogs I've had than from reading all the books I've read. Grouse hunting is quite different from quail hunting. With quail, you know where to go, but with grouse, the dog knows and you don't: he can get the air scent of a grouse, so you should just follow him. The average person figures he knows where he's going, but it's the wrong place. A person can't smell like a dog. And you don't train the dog as much as you train the owner: a dog can be fully trained, but if the owner doesn't know how to handle him and give the right commands, he's useless.

I stopped bird hunting when my legs gave out about three years ago, so I'm not going to go like a friend of mine did. He was quite a bit younger than I am—fifty-one years old, I believe—and they found him dead in the woods from a stroke. He'd shot his sixty-second bird that season.

72

"Groundhogs are good eating."

BOB MANN *is a retired photographer who drives a cab and does security work around Nashville, Tennessee. He is pictured with one of his groundhog-hunting guns, a .22 Magnum rifle.*

I don't like to hunt anything that's not to eat. Game animals were put on earth for man to eat, and it's a waste to kill them for no reason. Even groundhogs—we kill so many of them that we can't eat 'em all, but I make sure we give 'em away; we don't just let them lay there. Colored people eat a lot of them; they boil them and barbecue them, like they do coon and squirrel. You've got to keep groundhogs down because they're real hard on farmers— they eat up all the leafy stuff in your garden and ruin your soybeans, and then cattle are always breaking their legs in their holes—so we hear word of a farm that's covered up with them, and we go thin them out. But we don't waste them.

Groundhogs are good eating. They're like deer; they're strictly vegetarian, and they'll only eat the tenderest of plants, so they're very clean animals. You can get a lot of meat off them, too. The best time to shoot them is the spring and early summer, because during the summer they stuff themselves to prepare for hibernation, and get so roly-poly fat that you have to parboil them to get at the lean meat.

I shoot groundhogs with a .222 pistol up to 75 yards. Between there and about 200 yards, I use a little Sako .222 bolt-action rifle, and from there on out I use a .300 Winchester Magnum. Also, me and my buddy had a rifle made for groundhog, a .257 Weatherby shooting a .25-caliber, ninety-grain hollow-point bullet out of a really long bull barrel—too heavy to carry around, and too long to fit cross- ways into my Volkswagen. We use it from a sandbag rest on the roof of the Volkswagen with a twenty-power Weaver silhouette scope. That gun shoots accurately anywhere from 25 yards to 875 yards: all you have to do is know the range, and dial it up. I've always liked to shoot my groundhogs by sitting in one spot and shooting different ranges, and that gun's just the ticket.

There's no shortage of groundhogs around here, or other game for that matter. We've got a good Game and Fish Department in Tennessee, and the game's been getting thicker since I moved here at the end of World War II— deer, wild boar, bear, dove, quail, turkey, rabbit—so if you're a good hunter, you can live off the game. I don't, 'cause I'm not much of a cook, but I know quite a few people around here that do; they don't buy meat in the store at all.

The meat's a lot better, too. They keep looking for the cause of cancer, and I really believe it's all the stuff we're eating, like the steroids and things they feed meat animals, and the water we drink. It seems to me like the whole environment is going to pot, and everything else is going with it. And then on top of all that you've got the prospect of nuclear war.

Which brings us back to groundhogs. I personally wouldn't want to survive a nuclear war—I'd like to go in the first wave—but if you were a survivalist, groundhogs would become real important to you. You couldn't possibly put up enough food in advance to take care of yourself if something like that happened, and groundhogs would be just about the only game left. They live in holes, just like you would be.

"You ever tried to kill a deer with a rock?"

FRANK DELEA *is an auto mechanic who lives in Hillsdale, New York. He is pictured teaching his daughter, Allison, to handle a shotgun.*

Growing up in this area it was super. When I was Allison's age you didn't need a license, nobody bothered you; you'd just go over the hill, and it was never a problem to go out and get a couple of partridges or pheasant. We ate everything we shot. Venison was on the table year round; if it wasn't that, it was hamburger and potatoes, and ham on Sundays. Partridge, pheasant, rabbit, squirrels—they were all treats.

It was a way of life, I guess. That's why, when we were ten or eleven and we'd take a day off from school to go hunting; you never got hollered at as long as you got a partridge or two or a couple of gray squirrels. But if you didn't shoot something, your parents had a fit.

My buddy down the road, my older brother, my younger brother—we always went together. Everybody had a gun. Shotguns, .22s, it didn't matter. Half the time you couldn't afford shells for the darn things anyway. You'd rummage around and find old buckshot or slugs or something—you'd be out shooting rabbits with buckshot. You'd aim high and hope you hit them with only one pellet. It's things like that that you remember.

But now it's real tight. When you go to hunt, the land's all posted, especially around here. You can't hunt; it's even hard to fish anymore. When you find an area you *can* go into, you're scared to death to go in there. In the state parks and stuff where they let you hunt—you go in there, and there's a guy behind every tree. Some of them shoot at noise, and that makes me real nervous.

I guess you can't really get mad about people posting their land, but a lot of it around here is city people who've come up and posted their land tight because they like the deer, they like to see them come out and eat underneath their apple tree in the back field. And the people don't realize that those three or four deer already ate up an acre of corn before they came to work over the apples. And the deer have become so overpopulated that now in this area they're smaller in size—about 100 or 110 pounds dressed, where they used to be 150 or 160.

Last year I got lucky; the one I shot was, oh, 190 pounds dressed. It was over a hundred yards, and I touched it off, and he stood right there and never moved. That was with a .22-250, and they put them down as quick as anything. I said, "Look at that! I never touched the sonofabitch!" I was getting ready to put another shell in when all of a sudden he just flopped, dropped right there. I'd hit him square, and it went in and broke his whole neck bone, so it killed all the nerves to his legs, yet he stood right there.

I went down there, and him and me had some tussle for about half an hour. You ever tried to kill a deer or knock him out with a rock? Don't. You ever tried to cut a deer's throat when he's still alive? You'd better believe, you can get hurt. You get him thrashing and kicking around, and as sharp as those hooves are, they'll cut your legs wide open, or your stomach. Finally I broke his lower jaw with a rock, and that got him enough so I could cut his throat—but even then he still thrashed around for another ten minutes. That's when a pistol would have come in handy.

"I've seen expressions on deers' faces that were very pointed."

THOMAS WILLIAMS *is a novelist* (Whipple's Castle, The Hair of Harold Roux), *a Senior Professor of English at the University of New Hampshire, and a lifetime hunter. He is pictured with his sixty-year-old Cogswell & Harrison shotgun.*

Shooting these animals has become a closed subject in the last twenty years. My reaction to criticism about it can be sweetly reasonable. It can be almost apologetic. It can be based on the fact that I came from a place and a family that had guns, and I've *always* had guns—in fact, I bought my first .22 for two quarter bills when I was about eight years old. But I can also get fairly irate about the subject. Then I start asking people if they eat meat, and if they do eat meat, have they ever gutted a pig, and could they? Or would they rather have the *Einsatzgruppen* do it for them, because they're too sensitive themselves?

I know what keeps animal populations alive. Hunters, unless they're commercial hunters, are probably the best thing for animal populations. The antihunting people are not against animal populations disappearing; they're against the one idea that a human being should be so brutal as to kill an animal. But they don't mind mosquito control, that sort of thing. It's so discriminatory, that attitude, that I mainly just ignore it.

I do suffer for my attitude. Can you be a serious novelist, and be criticized by the academic critics, and have an attitude toward hunting that isn't theirs? That's a big question. I've been attacked on this subject for many, many years.

I once wrote a story called "Goose Pond." It's probably my best-known story, and I remember the first review of it. It was in *The Kenyon Review,* by some critic who called himself "Huckleberry Squib" or something like that, and it said something like, "If one wants to read about the shooting and skinning of the deer with primitive instruments, one might be interested in this story."

It is becoming the standard attitude in print, and that includes local papers in rural hunting states. Also, a kind of ignorance is standard. For instance, there was an article on muzzle-loader shooting in the local daily where I live—and this is an area where many, many people hunt—they had one picture of a percussion lock on a gun, and they called it a flintlock. They don't care what kind it is. The gun carries with it its own moral definition, and therefore, why bother with details? That's more frightening than the mistake.

I think maybe this attitude started in the 1920s, when people like, say, Robert Benchley made a kind of fetish about being a "civilized man" because he couldn't open a can with a can opener. I see it in my students. Let somebody write a paper about how he went out in the woods with his uncle Zack and shot his first deer, and watch them freeze.

I don't think *my* attitude is closed at all. I've seen expressions on deers' faces which were very pointed and very intelligent, and what they were saying to me was that I was some kind of Ork, some kind of a monster. I don't blame them, because I wanted to eat them.

"I have had to chase some people down."

KATHY BEZOTTE *works as a conservation officer for the state of Michigan. She carries a standard police sidearm, the .38 Special Smith & Wesson revolver.*

When I was growing up I must have used my grandmother's .22 once or twice, but that was about it. The story with this "Sharpshooter" badge is that they have four badges—Expert, Master, Sharpshooter, and Marksman—and so "Sharpshooter" is only one step above "Marksman." But I can generally hit what I'm aiming at.

My job is to enforce the fish and game and conservation laws of the state of Michigan. My law-enforcement commission states that I can enforce all the criminal laws of the state, but generally we concentrate on fish and game and conservation.

Most of the laws we enforce are misdemeanors, but people take them very seriously. Killing a deer out of season or without a permit carries a mandatory five days in jail, and hey, let's face it, jails aren't very nice. The guys who are out doing this take it *very* seriously. It's the middle of the night most of the time, and you're a long way from anywhere, and sometimes they take off on foot or in a car, or resist in some way. I have had to chase some people down.

I've only used my gun on injured animals. I don't carry a rifle, so if the deer is up and moving, I don't usually bother with it. They're pretty resilient, anyway; we get deer run-ning around here on three legs, things like that. Sometimes they're hit by cars and injured that way, or—well, I've had to kill some that were wounded and were down, and they were going to die sometime anyway. Then you can get close enough to use the .38.

I've never had to use it on a person. Usually it's more a deterrent than anything else. That's the best way to think about it. It's a tool, I guess, like the handcuffs or the cars we use. If you think about it as something you're going to be going out and shooting people with, you're probably going to be doing that, and you're probably going to be in a lot of trouble.

I like to go out and shoot and practice now and then, but I'm not waiting for free time at the end of the day so I can go out and shoot, and I don't have a firearm of my own—our .38s are owned by the state. I think hunting's a good sport for people as long as they're aware of the ethics of it and it's not just a slaughter, as it so often is, but I don't feel any real personal desire to do it. When you're out in the woods all day checking up on hunters, the last thing you want to do is change into your hunting clothes and go out there again. The gunbelt is about fourteen pounds hanging on my waist, and it's nice to take it off at the end of the day.

"The ones you want to shoot are maybe sixty years old."

JOHN MAHER, *a Bel Air, California, investment banker, goes on safari in Africa whenever he can. He is pictured in his living room with his favorite safari rifle, a pre-1964 Winchester Model 70 in .375 H&H caliber.*

A lot of the mythology of the African safari is real. You *do* hear the game during the night. You hear the lions roar and the leopards cough.

The kind of noise lions make is indescribable. They don't sound like they do in the zoo. It's a thrill. On your first safari on the first night, they're two miles away, and in that clear air they sound like they're in the latrine. They really do. You think they're right there, and "Where's the gun?" Then all of a sudden it's five or six o'clock in the morning and the native is there outside your tent politely clearing his throat to act as the local alarm clock, and he whispers "Bwana?" It's terrific. I mean, that's a good way to start the day.

And hunting isn't just killing, you know. Killing's easy. I've been involved in hunts with people who did that, just stacked as many trophies around the camp as they could, flashed their tape measures around the place, and that's just a bore.

The particular attraction to me is with the "dangerous" game. The fact that you've done it right (the stalk and kill) and that it's a quality trophy representative of the species is a real high. You get a different feeling shooting an elephant than you do shooting a cat, because elephants are, so to speak, higher in the strata of species than the cats. They're highly intelligent animals, and the ones you want to shoot are maybe sixty years old, so that's a really important event. That's really something with a very bittersweet quality. I've made a conscious decision not to shoot another elephant unless one of its tusks weighs a hundred pounds. To me, that's the ultimate trophy.

But cats, particularly lions, are different. They're predators. They're mean animals. When you're driving back into camp, for instance, the blacks get very excited if you've knocked down a cat, and they get more excited about a lion than anything else. The lion is in the back of the car, and it's a big lion with a big mane, and the wind's in your face and the car's going down the road, it's Africa, you're a zillion miles from anywhere, nobody can get you on the phone, and these guys start singing. I mean, there's a little bit of romance left in life, you know?

This is a romantic event, a truly romantic event. To the typical bush native, a lion represents a real potential threat to his existence, so when one is shot, it's an event, a real event, and they react. These people's emotions are so basic and so sincere and so strong. Their faces are open. And you as the perpetrator—well, "perpetrator" may be the wrong word; maybe "crusader" is better, but that's too strong the other way—you get caught up in it. And these people like to make sure the lion is dead. The kids go over and give it a little kick, throw a little sand in its face and so forth, get a little macho.

When that happens, you can be a damn cynical, sophisticated business type and *still* be excited. Damn excited.

"I get flak from both sides."

OTIS CHANDLER *is Chairman of the Board and Editor-in-Chief of The Times Mirror Company in Los Angeles, a champion trophy hunter, and a vocal supporter of handgun control. He is pictured in his office in front of a photograph of his trophy room.*

I get flak from both sides. I get it from my hunting friends, who say, "I thought you were one of us, a good guy, a patriotic American who believes in the right to bear arms guaranteed in the Bill of Rights. You must be influenced by all those liberal editors of yours, or you've got a screw loose." They cannot understand how I can be a hunter and also be for gun registration. Then I'm given a hard time by people in the urban areas who don't like people who "murder" animals.

I try to answer these people. At the drop of a hat I will try to articulate the major points about why sport hunting, which is what I do, is a moral and justifiable avocation.

Sport hunting enhances the animal population. The money that I pay for licenses and tags and sales taxes on ammunition and guns and gun products goes to the preservation of species and habitats—not one income-tax dollar is used for that. Then there's the fact that of all game animals that are legally licensed to be taken in the world, only one per cent die because of legal hunting. In most areas of the world where there is a problem with an animal's survival, poaching is the number-one issue. I was the last person to hunt the tiger legally in India in '71; now the game wardens and game biologists who used to protect the tiger when hunting was legal are not in place, and there's no careful management of the animal population. It's open season for poachers. You can look at two or three hundred skins of freshly killed tigers in Calcutta if you know the right phone number. The point is that with legal sport hunting comes careful management of animal populations with as much preservation of habitats as we are able to achieve.

On the other front, the people who are against gun registration only quote half of the statement in the Bill of Rights. They quote the "right to bear arms" bit, but they leave out the bit that says "in order to form a people's militia."

They argue that if you and I are called out on the village square to join a people's militia, we won't have a handgun because it's been confiscated. And if it's been confiscated, "they" will take over. Well, who are "they"? The handgun people don't explain that issue. If you're going to first call out our trained forces in an emergency—the Army, the Navy, the Air Force, the Marines, and the National Guard —and then the people's militia, I would say that the latter group would not be critical to our national survival. If they want us citizens to come out and try to save the country after all our forces are gone, I predict that the country's finished.

Then people say that you have to have a gun because you're liable to be attacked by some kind of criminal element. On that score, I've talked to a number of sensible law-enforcement people who say that you're better off without a gun. The person who is threatening you or violating the privacy of your office or your home or your car or wherever is highly charged, maybe on drugs, and if you confront him or her with a weapon, particularly a gun, they are liable to do you great bodily damage, like blow you away. Whereas, if you appear to be calm and don't threaten them, they may leave you alone after they rob you or whatever. That makes sense to me.

And really, I think registration is a fairly simple thing. We're asked to register our cars, our boats, our airplanes, our dogs, our cats, our bicycles and motorcycles—what have I forgotten?—so what's the big deal about registering your gun once a year and paying the three bucks?

84

"The police just knocked on the door and then went away."

RICHARD T. ADKINSON, *a sport-pistol shooter, has been a probation officer and a juvenile-prison superintendent. Currently he is Chief of Employee Relations of the District of Columbia and an adviser to the District of Columbia Chief of Police.*

This has never been a "gun town," so it's easy for the politicians and the bureaucrats, most of whom are very anti-gun, to confuse people. The District has about the most repressive gun laws in the country, and also one of the highest crime rates, and the local politicians would have us believe that the anti-gun laws somehow keep the crime rate down.

I think, however, that people are beginning to approach the matter logically. In a vote on an initiative two years ago, for instance, 75 percent of the popular vote was in favor of mandatory sentences for people using a gun in the commission of a violent felony. That, not the denial of guns to the citizenry, is the way to connect antigun and anticrime legislation.

The problem, in my view, lies largely with the courts, and there were two cases here in D.C. which perfectly illustrated our points. The first was an outrageous and somewhat infamous case in which a teenager broke into the NRA building, stole a weapon belonging to one of the employees, then went out and killed somebody. The estate of the victim sued the NRA, and they won two million dollars in a local court.

That's how the courts treated that issue. The kid was a different story. He was fifteen, and this was his second murder; his first was when he was twelve, a little old lady up around Dupont Circle. That kid knew that the most he was going to get was two years. What did he have to fear?

The decision in the second case was a landmark, because it established that the police have no duty to protect the individual citizen. There were three women who heard somebody trying to force their way into their apartment, and called the police. Meanwhile, the attackers forced their way through the door. One of the women hid, but the other two were raped.

While all of this was going on, the police arrived. But the one woman who was hiding couldn't call out, so the police just knocked on the door and then went away. Hearing them go away, the concealed woman called the police a second time. They came back, but all they did was cruise the block.

The attackers heard the woman when she made that second call, so all three women got rather brutally raped and sodomized. When the men had raped them so much that they couldn't do it any more, they made the women perform perverted acts on each other. The whole thing kept up for about fourteen hours. And when the women sued, the court held that the police had no responsibility to protect them; their only duty was to "the maintenance of public order."

Now, in a city where the law also forbids you to own a gun for self-protection, where does that leave you? The people here are no longer going to tolerate that kind of stuff.

"In Russia, even your knives and forks have to be blunt."

IVAN TROFIMOV *is the son of a Russian immigrant to the United States. An engineering consultant, he lives near Dayton, Ohio.*

The most interesting gun I have is this Mauser .25 pistol, 1896 Model. My father was issued one—I don't know if this one I've got now was the one, but if it wasn't, the one he had was its twin—along with a larger Mauser, the 9-millimeter with the case you used as a stock to make it a carbine. This .25 is the "night-pin" gun; if there's a round in the chamber, this little pin comes out and you can feel a bump on the side of the gun. It got valuable around 1955, when they realized that there weren't many of them around anymore.

My father was a submarine commander in the Russian Imperial Navy in 1917. He was just a kid, twenty-two, the youngest full commander they had. He was on the First Soviet Council at Kronstadt—what did *he* know about politics? *He* was out torpedoing German ships when the Czar abdicated—and he was told there to take his three submarines to Finland, then report back to do a mapping of the harbor.

Well, he knew that they didn't really want him to map the harbor, and sure enough, when he got to Finland, his bosun's mate came into his cabin and said, "Captain, you're here because you're delivering the submarines, but you're not supposed to show up again. We are assigned to do you in."

That kind of thing was happening all over the place, but the bosun said, "Skipper, you've been with us all through the war, and we're damned if we're going to do *anything* to you. Here's some money, here's some clothes. Hop in this boat out here."

They got him into open country and in touch with some people, and he went all the way across Russia and Siberia to Japan, then to this country. It took him a year, and he had the .25 with him all the time.

One time, he told me, he got off a train to go to the toilet in the bushes, and suddenly some Red Guards appeared, all in a shambles as they were, just ruffians. One of them had a rifle, he told me, and one had a pistol. He said, "What would *you* do?"

I guess I didn't know, I was a kid, so he said, "Well, you should always shoot the guy with the pistol first, because it takes time to get your hands on a rifle and swing it around. By knocking off the guy with the pistol first, you've gained maybe a second or two seconds before you have to get the guy with the rifle." But he didn't have to do it. The Red Guards fell into some other conversation, and he got back on the train.

He was pretty sure that he was well disguised, that they didn't know he was an officer. They just butchered officers. They'd take their bodies into the nearest town, and leave their coats and epaulets on. Then they'd cut off their pants and string them up by the balls. Anyone who touched the corpse would be shot.

So now the ruffians are running Russia, and what have the Russian people got to defend themselves against them? In Russia, even your knives and forks have to be blunt, or you're off to the Gulag.

Here, if the National Guard was told to take over this town, they'd think twice. It might cost them some casualties.

"The .45 is the best system in the world."

MIKE DALTON *is a champion IPSC shooter who teaches self-defense with a handgun at the International Shootists Institute in Los Angeles.*

In IPSC shooting, you learn to shoot a powerful handgun quickly and accurately. It's one of the few dual-purpose sports. It's sort of like swimming: in swimming, you can enjoy your pool and have a lot of fun recreationally, and when you're out in the middle of the ocean and your boat sinks, you have a chance to save your life.

At ISI we teach people how to handle themselves and their weapons in a life-threatening situation. We begin by teaching them how to handle a gun in a totally safe manner, then we go on to the choice of equipment for defensive use.

For people who are interested in shooting recreationally, or who just want to go visit the range once or twice a month, we recommend a four-inch-barrel .38 Special revolver, double-action variety, made by a good manufacturer like Colt or Ruger or Smith & Wesson. That type of weapon is very safe to operate and very quick to get into action, and it has a very controllable recoil. It's a good compromise. With modern hollow-point ammunition you get respectable stopping power.

For people who want a semi-automatic handgun and are able to shoot once a week or more, we recommend the .45 Colt or Randall Service models. That's because they are better systems than the .38 once they have been tested and tuned. You need to put more time and effort into learning how to handle a .45, but once you've mastered it, it's faster than a revolver, it holds more ammunition, and that big bullet works very well.

Out of the box, straight from the manufacturer, the revolver is more dependable than the semi-automatic. The reason is that generally, semi-automatics are manufactured to fire ball ammunition; usually, they are not machined to take hollow-point, soft-point, or semi-wadcutter ammunition, and they are likely to jam if you use these types of bullets—which are the kinds of bullets you should use. Once properly modified, however, the .45 is the best system in the world.

After we have taught our people about safety and equipment, we teach them the basics of grip and sighting and so on, then we teach them how to handle dangerous confrontation situations—when to shoot, how to use cover, how to evaluate situations so that they shoot the right person or persons, and how to stay alive. Then we teach them the legal aspects of self-defense with a handgun. Our lawyer makes all that very plain.

Another thing we teach is to avoid the situation if at all possible. For instance, if you know that somebody's out in your living room unplugging your television set, stay in your room. You can replace your television set, but you can't replace your life. Also, you should keep your bedroom door locked. That way, somebody's going to have to make noise to get in there. If they get in, you've got the gun and you know how to use it.

We don't look at this like we're training a bunch of John Waynes who are going to go out and clean up the world. That's not realistic. After just a few days of instruction, no matter how good, these people are not *ready* to clean up the world. They'll be doing well just to keep themselves alive. That's what we strive for.

"He was maybe two and a half pounds away from eternity."

JERRY PREISER *is a gun dealer, range owner, and lobbyist/ spokesman for New York State gun owners. His favorite weapon is a customized 1911 Model A-1 Colt .45 semi-automatic.*

I always carry. If I'm going out on a weekend with the wife and I want to wear something a little more comfortable than the .45, I might swap into a Model 36 Smith & Wesson, a .38 five-shot little tiny revolver. I can tuck that into my waistband or something. But generally speaking, I have *supreme* confidence in the .45.

I have a gun with me even when I'm taking a crap. When I'm sitting on the toilet, that .45 is literally six or seven inches from my hand. So while I take it off when I go to move my bowels, that gun is still there. You have to have access to it because the one time you don't have the gun, just sure as shit, that's gonna be the time you need it—you know, "Wait here, I'll be right back, I have to go to my apartment."

This is a great personal weapon because the .45 is a heavy bullet. It's not a fast bullet. You can go to a .22 or a .223, varmint-type guns, high-velocity guns, and the shock of the hit might kill a guy, but the .45 is a slow-moving bullet, a big, fat, heavy slug, and no matter where you hit a guy, you'll stop him. This gun, you see, was developed when we were fighting the Morros in the Philippines, and those guys were so hopped-up that even if you hit them a couple of times, they'd still have enough to take you. Among sophisticated aficionados of the gun, the .45 is the ideal cartridge for stopping a guy, short of going to some-thing outrageous like a .357 or a .44 Magnum. There are problems when you go that hot, see. Now you're going to a fat slug that's traveling *fast,* as opposed to a fat slug that's moving slow. It can go through you and hit that Minnie across the street, and maybe even ricochet around and do God knows what. So there's a limit to the desirable range of that cartridge; you don't want it to just keep on doing damage, and the .45 is a happy compromise. It works.

They have all kinds of sophisticated loads for this gun now. I'm shooting a silvertip. There's a high content of silver alloy in there. She's also a hollow-head; she's been beveled out, so when she hits you, it's gonna be controlled. It's gonna go in, and then she's gonna mushroom out, so in addition to that heavy shock, that knock-down punch, she's gonna open you. The arm? Off. So you don't *need* more than that.

The silvertip is my normal load. I could be humane and carry hardball loads, regular army issue, and I could group nicely and drill nice neat holes, but in the excitement of combat I might drill the nice neat holes and the guy might still keep coming. Still shooting at me, as it were.

I only ever pulled once. Eight or nine years ago, in a park-yourself garage. Late at night, and I'm up on the third or fourth level, and a black gentleman comes up behind me as I'm getting into my car. I drew, and I didn't have to shoot—but the safety was off, and there was a little pressure on the trigger. He was maybe two and a half pounds away from eternity.

"You've got at least a fifty-fifty chance of surviving."

PAUL DUMONT *lives in a semirural area of New Hampshire. An entrepreneur and salesman, he was in the wood-burning-stove business at the time of the interview.*

I think everyone should know how to shoot a gun, because I think we live in a false sense of security. People shouldn't really feel as secure as they do. You take an animal in the woods—its senses are keen, and it's aware of its enemies; it knows it *has* enemies. But a lot of people, especially Americans, feel safe in their houses, and they think they'll never need a gun, and besides, guns are evil. Why are humans safe? Tell me. Are *you* safe?

I mean, anything can happen. The Russians could come over here. People flip out and do crazy things. People get up in towers, and some of them are ex-Marines, and they start picking people off. Your cities run out of food for some reason or other, and people say, "Let's hit the countryside," come driving by here, say "Hey, *there's* a place, it's out in the country, let's shoot the whole fuckin' family." Nobody's gonna hear anything. You could shoot all night out here, and nobody would come. What are you gonna do? Who's gonna help you?

If that happens to me and they get in the door, they ain't gonna get upstairs. I've got maybe five thousand rounds up there. If I run out of bullets, they're probably gonna be out, too. If you've got a gun and you know how to use it, you've got at least a fifty-fifty chance of surviving. A lot of people have died because they didn't have that fifty-fifty chance. If the other guy has a gun, it's no goddam good at all to wave a fireside implement at him, is it?

I try to shoot once a week, and when I do, I go through four or five hundred rounds. I use different guns different times. A lot of times in the morning I don't feel like carrying a rifle, so I'll go out with one of my pistols. Other times, like on a Sunday, I'll go out with four or five guns. I'd love to have a full-automatic weapon, but they're hard to get.

I like all the guns in different ways. I like the looks of my .30-30. I like that western look. I like that .357 Smith & Wesson because you can blast it off real fast—pow-pow-pow! I like my semi-automatic .22s because you can do a lot of shooting. Probably my favorite overall is my Remington pump shotgun. You can squeeze it off real fast, but you *really* get a blast. I get in different moods. One day I like one gun, another day I like another. My wife's a real good shot, too. Sometimes she's even better than me.

A lot of my friends disapprove of guns, won't have them in the house, but to each his own. They don't like me having them, but they don't give me no shit about it. Ha! People in general don't give me much shit about anything.

I keep the guns in the bedroom, with the ammunition. I keep that .357 with six shells right next to it all the time. There's another one that's *always* loaded, too. You haven't seen that one; that's the one I'm not showing you.

"This guy started showing up, 'Crazy Larry'."

INGRID COOPERMAN *moved recently from New York City to rural Vermont, where most of the time she lives alone with her children. She is pictured with her 12-gauge pump shotgun.*

The first gun we got was the .22, and I think that was just to be like everybody else. Everybody had some sort of gun, and we wanted to show that we weren't city folk, we weren't summer folk, we weren't tourists, we were *real people!*

So the .22 just sort of sat there. That's not a real *weapon* weapon anyway. It's more something you'd use for squirrels, isn't it? But that's the only one that ever gets used. Sometimes when city guys come up, Mort will take them out with it—you know, *ha ha ha, country life!*—and they'll shoot at soda cans or something.

But what I regard as the *weapons* weapons, the shotgun and the automatic pistol, came when I had my leg in a splint, and I had to take care of the kids, and Mort was in the city, and suddenly this guy started showing up—"Crazy Larry." He's sort of nuts, and he would trespass very freely and say sort of alarming things. The police were strange about it. On the one hand they seem benevolently amused by it and say, "Oh, that's just Crazy Larry," but then they'd say he'd just got out of prison for attempted arson and he beats up his family. The one time I called them for help, they called back in an hour for directions.

So I was thinking, what could I do if something turned ugly? I couldn't run—my leg was in a splint. I couldn't yell for help—nobody would hear me. If I called the police, the same thing would happen again.

So in a fit of paranoia I went off to Bob's Gun Shop and bought the shotgun and the automatic. Then we got very frightened that we had these dangerous things lying about, so we sort of separated the ammunition from the guns. I don't even *know* where the ammunition for the .22 is. I think the buckshot for the shotgun is over in the little house somewhere. The pistol's the only one which is accessible at all, and that with some difficulty.

I don't know how to load the shotgun. As far as I know, it's never been fired. But that may be one of the most dangerous things, to have guns about and not know how to use them. It seems sort of silly. It seems that either I should get rid of them entirely, or really learn how to know what I'm doing and even teach the kids to know what they're doing.

The local people think we're crazy to live here as we do. All the women down in the village say, "I could never live like that. I'd be terrified, especially if my husband wasn't there all the time." They've lived here all their lives, and we're newcomers, so maybe they know something we don't.

"It's my buddy."

Louise Blair *helps her husband run the Sagebrush Inn near Taos, New Mexico. It was he who bought her the .38 Special revolver she holds in the photograph.*

I was a schoolteacher before I met my husband, who owned the inn. He's a very artistic person who likes to work with natural elements like adobe, but he also has respect for danger, and he taught me to respect it too. I had never had anything to do with guns before I met him, but now, when he's not here, my gun is practically my best friend. It goes with me from room to room.

We live in an extremely remote, large house on a mud road. It's a bad road, but it's a shortcut, so a lot of people use it, and they're always getting stuck in the middle of the night. They come here then. We've had everything from Mexicans who are hiding from the Border Patrol to movie stars who have bottomed out their Cadillacs. When the doorbell rings, I answer it with the gun in my hand.

I've had to ask people not to come in the door, and I've had to show them the gun. Usually, that happens when they're really drunk, and it happens maybe four or five times a year. People under the influence of drugs or alcohol do not have much judgment, so just telling them to go away often doesn't work. Showing them the gun works, though; I've never had an incident which escalated beyond my showing the gun.

I'd only shoot it if somebody were actually lunging at me or breaking in through the big windows we have; then, I wouldn't hesitate. It's not like I could call the police and have them show up right away, and I don't think women can handle knives effectively, and I'm not a judo expert, and often when my husband isn't here, he takes the dog with him. I can scream really loudly, but what good would that do me? It's not as if there were neighbors who could hear me screaming, or even shooting: we have no neighbors. My husband has rifles in the house, but I can't shoot them, so that leaves the pistol.

I've shot it maybe three or four times in my whole life, and it's really loud. The first time I shot it, I shook so hard that I nearly dropped it—but now that I haven't heard that loud sound in so many years, it's just like, "Oh yeah—pick it up and carry it with me." It's automatic. It's a pretty gun, too; it's nicely plated and it has pearl handles and everything. It's my buddy.

I must add that I am not at all interested in using a gun under any circumstances for hunting or injuring an animal unless it were attacking me, like a rabid skunk. I'm not a "gun person" at all. But if you live in the boonies, you just have to have a gun and be ready to use it. Otherwise, don't live in the boonies.

"You know when you're going to be held up."

Thomas McCaffrey *owns an antique jewelry store in Chicago. He keeps five handguns concealed around his store. One of them is the .380 Llama pistol on his desk.*

I've always had long guns, but I bought my first handgun when my wife was held up in the store. It dawned on me that people were just wandering around the streets with guns, and we were sitting here like the little ducks in the machines at the amusement park. We'd go round and round, and they'd take potshots at us. So I thought I'd reverse that psychology a bit. We may be little ducks going around, but we're armed ducks that'll shoot back.

I'm not out to start a gunfight in the store. It's just that in certain businesses, you give them the $500 in the till, and let it go. You don't have to worry about it. But in the jewelry business, I might have $150,000 or $200,000 or more in other people's jewelry here, and then I have an inventory of over a quarter of a million dollars, so I've got a lot to lose.

You know when you're going to be held up. At least six times a year, we are positively in the process of being held up. We know what's going down. Two men will come into the store, then another man will come in, then maybe another, and then one man will go outside, and there may be a car parked there. These people are just roaming around the store, looking at the camera, looking into the back room, and they always want to know "How much is this watch? How much is *this* one?"—looking for the most expensive stuff. So we know what's going down.

We have remote radio holdup buttons and stationary holdup buttons, and we have the camera, and we get a four- or five-minute response from the police, so we have a certain way of running the store and putting these things into operation when something's coming down, and if it gets really heavy, I usually just take one of my pistols and stick it right down the front of my pants where they can see it, and I stand in the doorway at the back of the store with my hand on the pistol, and I just look at 'em.

One time when we were being set up, my wife actually saw this one guy's gun in his shoulder holster when he was leaning over one of the display cases. I'd been out somewhere, and when I came in the atmosphere was electric; people's eyes were bugging out, and it was really hot. My wife was waiting on this guy—there were five of them in the store—and she excused herself and went in the back and called the cops, then came out again.

I'd gone into the back room and got my pistol out, and I was behind the door where I thought they couldn't see me, just waiting for this guy to draw his gun, but they must have seen me through the crack in the door, because all of a sudden they just *fled*. They were out of the store in, oh, maybe three and a half seconds.

I was going to nail the guy on the spot. Just nail him. I wasn't going to ask him to put down his weapon. That would just have led to gunfire. If he'd drawn the gun, I would have shot him.

"I take 'em off when I bathe and go to bed."

"WILDMAN" DENT MYERS *owns a Civil War memorabilia store in Kennesaw, Georgia. He wears two revolvers, a .44 Special Charter Arms Bulldog and a .357 Colt Lawman III, on his belt.*

Some guns from the War Between the States, like the LeMatt pistol, are extremely rare. Confederate weapons in particular are hard to find, because a lot of them were confiscated and destroyed after the war, and also because people seem to have a natural bent for collecting the weapons of so-called "conquered" groups.

Under the circumstances, Confederate guns were pretty high quality. We had no manufacturing facilities at all in this area (all the factories were up North), so during the four years of the war we had to set up the manufacturing of screws and bolts and castings and forgings—everything we needed. We did pretty good: in four years, we accomplished what had taken the United States two hundred years. Then of course we bought a lot of weapons in Europe: the LeMatts from France, the Whitworths from England, and so on. Those Whitworths were no slouch. They had telescopic sights and hexagonal barrels, and they registered kills at eighteen hundred yards. We made some good Yankee officers with those guns.

We were the only ones that had 'em. The English Queen and Parliament were on our side because of our cotton, so there was a lot of trading, but England was officially on the Yankee side because of *Uncle Tom's Cabin.* That book sold more copies in England than it did here, and the common workers related to the poor old downtrodden niglets.

When I was little, I wasn't even aware that there had been a War Between the States. I was raised back up in the sticks, and my folks were sharecroppers about three grades lower than the niglets, so I didn't know nothin'. I only found out about the war around 1950, when I started digging stuff up. This area is rich in history, see. It's where they captured "The General"—the train, that is—and at one time about a hundred thousand Yankees jumped down the ridge and met about sixty-eight thousand of us, and lost a bunch of stuff. I dug some of it up, and then I started reading the histories and got hooked. Now I kinda consider this store my school; I learn more every day from the people who come in here. I even had the King of Afghanistan in here one time; he made me a major in the Afghanistan Army.

I don't wear my guns all the time: I take 'em off when I bathe and go to bed. Mainly they're a deterrent; I never take 'em out of their holsters except to clean 'em or use them, and I only used one once. A guy in a Dempsey Dumpster tried to run over me and my dog, and by automatic reaction (I didn't do it on purpose), I pulled and blew his windshield out, busted his drive train, all that kind of stuff. I went and told the sheriff, and nothing came of it.

When I was a kid, my family was so low on the scale that the niglets wouldn't let us play with them. Now I have nothing against 'em except when somebody arbitrarily forces them into my company. I'm not a violent person by nature—don't believe in violence—but I do believe in my city, my county, my state, my country, and the Confederacy, not necessarily in that order.

"We use our guns to scare people that we're visiting."

Peggy Parson is Klaliff of the Cullman County, Alabama Ku Klux Klan. Before it was disbanded, she was a member of the Klan Special Forces unit charged with the protection of Invisible Empire chief Bill Wilkinson.

We receive a lot of threats from blacks and Jews and different groups, so we need to be armed. I believe in the right to bear arms, even to the point where I think that if blacks want to own guns, they should be able to. It would be just as wrong for us to take their guns as it would be for them to try to take ours. So let 'em have 'em. It'll probably end in a race war like that, but . . .

There's only about one percent blacks in Cullman County, though. Until a few years ago, there was a sign at the train depot in the middle of town: "Nigger, don't let the sun set on you," with a nigger dummy hanging from a hangman's noose. That sign meant what it said. Now, they move in, but usually the Klan doesn't do anything 'cause it could be a setup. The Feds have done so much of that, that now there's always the suspicion. We've really quieted down on that lately, then.

We do a lot of other things that need to be done, though, with whites as well as blacks. For instance, we've had several problems where the police haven't been able to do anything about drug dealers, and they've come to us. We would run 'em out of town or, y'know, whatever. And quite a few parents who can't do anything with their kids—eighteen-year-olds who are past the age where they have to listen to Mom and Daddy, but are still living at home and really running wild—they'll call us and ask us to throw a scare into 'em, and we do.

Anytime the Klan goes out to visit somebody and they don't straighten up, they'll go back and whip 'em with hickories. They don't use anything but hickories. It cuts, and nine out of ten people have to crawl away when it's finished. Those people really don't need for the Klan to come back. Sometimes the Klan doesn't give no warning, like with child molesters.

We use our guns to scare people that we're visiting, like we mean business. And we do. It really scares people to have a loaded gun pointed right at their head.

This kind of work can get dangerous, too. Like, this one time we went out to beat this man who'd been forcing his wife to write bad checks and selling food stamps, then getting on the C.B. and begging for food. Everybody had their job, and mine was to cut the porch lights and keep his three children in the house.

Well, the "children" turned out to be three boys between the ages of sixteen and twenty-one, and a younger child, and the man's wife. I'm cutting the porch light while the men are off beating this man, and the biggest of the three boys comes out and pulls a knife out, and sticks it up to my belly. I'm five foot ten, and I'm looking up at this "child."

Without my gun, that would have been bad trouble. Even after I pulled it and had it right on him he ran into the house looking for a gun in there, and I had to stop him and hold all of them for twenty minutes while those six guys whipped on one man outside.

I got quite a reputation out of that incident. I held those boys for twenty minutes. And they knew I wasn't foolin'. I never pull a gun unless I intend to use it. I've used it before, and if anyone tries to harm me or my family, I'll use it again.

"The bullet had taken off the ball of his earlobe."

TOMMY REESNOVER *acts as a bodyguard for Nashville* Tennessean *reporter* JERRY THOMPSON *(rear). His presence results from threats made against Thompson by the Ku Klux Klan following his undercover infiltration and exposé of that organization.*

TOMMY: I keep my gun here with me in the store, but Jerry doesn't like me to carry it when I'm around him, so I don't. Besides, it's a lot of trouble. We went to Canada one time, and you don't carry no short pistols in Canada; that sort of thing, and airplanes. It's just a hassle, a real hassle.

Jerry and I go back a long way, and I like to call myself his "traveling companion." Not "bodyguard"; Jerry can take care of himself just as well as I can take care of myself. I knew he wasn't gonna run and I knew I wasn't gonna run, so I made a deal with him: I'd take the first one. At least, that's what I told him . . .

But the main thing about being a bodyguard is instinct. Like when we were in Pittsburgh and those Nazis walked in, I knew they were trouble. We handled it well, Jerry in his way and I in mine, and they didn't prevent him from talking. I didn't need no gun for that.

JERRY: I really don't like to be around guns, and I especially don't like to be around Tommy and guns. I really don't want him to carry a gun when he's with me.

You want to know why? All right: I'll tell you a little anecdote about Tommy and guns.

As Tommy told you, we go back a long way, so I can't remember exactly when this happened, but one night we've been in this after hours bar across from the newspaper office, and as we're leaving at about 2 A.M.—me alone in my car and Tommy and a bail bondsman and another friend behind me—these two fellers see me coming out of the alley, alone in the car, and they're going to murder me!

Of course, I know that I have three hosses behind me to back me up, so I just get out to make my stand. Before this one guy on the other side of the car can get around, Tommy sees what's going on, and he's there. These guys are in a fight.

I've caught my man in the car door, so I'm trying to pummel him a little when I see Tommy hit his guy upside the head with this little pistol he's got. Right then I see this big streak of fire, and I just know it's gone right through the guy's damned head. I run right around the car—"You all right, buddy? You hurt?"—but fortunately, the round has gone over his head and ricocheted off the building.

Those guys left in one hell of a hurry, and that was that. It wasn't until two weeks later, when I met the bail bondsman on the street—we lost him that night—that we found out that Tommy's bullet had taken off the ball of his earlobe after it ricocheted off the building.

He said, "I'll never go with you crazy sons of bitches ever again, anywhere!" He hasn't, either.

That's when I started to worry about Tommy and guns. Another time, he shot three holes in a Pabst Blue Ribbon beer sign in a bar, all the way down the length of this long, narrow, crowded bar—talk about a crowded stairwell! Those people left in a hurry!—and I think that's when *he* started to worry about him and guns.

TOMMY: Well, in the first instance, the gun I hit that feller with was a .25 automatic, and those things are always going off accidentally. It wasn't my fault. I was carrying it because of "ease of concealment." In the second case, well, that was just a damn good feeling.

"This rumor got around about me shooting this guy."

C. F. MONROE, *a retired paving contractor, was encountered at a gun show in Gaylord, Michigan, where he was selling part of his extensive gun collection.*

Why am I selling these guns? I'm selling them 'cause I'm seventy-six, don't look forward to a whole lot of years, and Michigan is a bad place to have anything of great value right now.

We live in the country, and I have two well-trained police dogs. I had one before that, but they poisoned it. Had to have it destroyed. So, I don't like to shoot people, though I did shoot one. He got twenty-seven Number Sixes in his back and rear end.

He was a well-known window-peeker in a little town called Peary, Michigan. They caught him in Peary, so he started riding a bicycle out in the country. 'Course I didn't know him from a bowl of apples, but he was on the porch and he tried the door. I was sitting there watching television with the lights out, see, late at night, but I seen his silhouette against these lights on a tower about a half a mile from the house—saw him when he moved and covered up the lights.

I got up and whispered to the wife, "Don't get excited if you hear me shooting, 'cause I'm going to scare the hell out of somebody, or capture him if he gets in the house." But what he done is just tried the outside door, is all.

So I went down the stairs—my guns are all in the basement, see—and picked up a Browning automatic and put two shells in. He could see the basement stairs, so I was yawning as I went down, like I was going to bed or some-thing, but when I came up he saw the gun, and he started running. I was barefoot, and I chased him across a gravel drive, hollered "Stop!" and shot once over his head. Next time I pulled down on him— "You're just a nice good range"—and took him right off his feet, probably more from shock than anything else. He was pretty well stung. He ran off in the weeds.

I called the Sheriff's Department and they come, of course, their lights aflashin' and their sirens blowin' for two miles coming in, driving like hell, and they run right past our place and had to back up. Meantime, the fella got up and ran across a crack-grass field. You can track him in it, of course, 'cause he cracks it right down, see.

Anyway, this old fella had to go have the shot pulled out of him, so they turned him in to the State Police. But then they didn't prosecute me, so nothing happened to me. You shoot a man in the road, you're liable to get prosecuted. You don't know if he's coming for gasoline, or if he's a drunk walking home, or *what* he's doing, see. Anyway, that was that.

This rumor got around about me shooting this guy. It didn't come out for about a year who it was I shot, but they knew I shot somebody. The Sheriff's Department are great noisemakers, see. But shortly after that, these people start driving by, looking at all the houses. We live on a three-mile road, and every house on the road has been broken into, except mine. All the mailboxes have been kicked over, except mine. I mean *all* of them, except mine.

108

"You have a right to defend your life against people who want to end it."

WARREN CASSIDY *is Director of the Institute For Legislative Action, the arm of the National Rifle Association that fights local and national gun-control legislation.*

I think that in the statistics—not NRA statistics, but figures from police and other sources totally independent of this organization—we have irrefutable proof that over 99 percent of all the legally owned shotguns, rifles, and handguns manufactured and sold in this country are never used in the commission of any crime.

Next, we have additional evidence that three quarters of those who commit violent crimes with or without guns have a series of arrests on their records prior to their commission of the ultimate violent crime.

After you read these statistics, you have to ask yourself how anybody could come up with the thought that by banning the guns used and owned and collected by the law-abiding citizen, you could lower the crime rate.

You see, federal law prohibits a felon from legally buying a gun, and should he somehow be able to circumvent the law and buy a gun from a registered dealer, that gun can eventually be traced to him. Therefore he pays a fee to the underworld for a gun which has been rendered untraceable in some fashion. That will exist no matter what new laws come onto the books, so really, how on earth can the elimination of gun ownership by the law-abiding citizen stop the use of guns in violent crime?

The major group proposing the restriction or banning of private ownership of guns in this country is the mavens of the media: the television and radio people, and the people who own major metropolitan newspapers. Those people have adopted what they believe to be the correct lifestyle that the American public should live. No private ownership of handguns is just one element in that lifestyle.

Now, these people are an elite—and when you're sitting up there in Westchester County behind electronic wrought-iron gates, you personally don't have to worry about survival. Those people know that they will be excluded from the consequences of the policies they advocate. They advocate forced busing, but their own children will never darken the door of a public school, and the same is true of their position on gun control. In fact, some of the publishers of those big newspapers—Sulzberger of the New York *Times,* for instance—have permits to carry concealed handguns while they editorialize against that right for the people.

The absolute bottom line on this issue, though, is that, if I remember my high school biology correctly, the primary human drive is air hunger. That translates into survival. You have a requirement to stay alive, and part of that is the right to defend your life against people who want to end it, if necessary with a gun. How anyone can argue against that right is beyond me.

110

"In the two and a half years we've had the law in force, we have had only one armed robbery."

DARVIN PURDY, *the Mayor of Kennesaw, Georgia, sponsored legislation requiring that an operable firearm and appropriate ammunition be kept in every household in that small town.*

There were three reasons for our law. Firstly, every state grants its people the right of self-defense, and without question a firearm is the most effective means of self-defense. Therefore we are equipping our citizens with the best means of taking care of themselves. Secondly, there were certain areas of the country passing antigun laws, and we wanted to show that there was a legal side of the gun issue other than confiscation. Thirdly, we thought that our law would serve as a deterrent to criminals contemplating coming into our area to commit criminal acts.

As soon as the law was passed, the media arrived on our doorsteps in droves. That certainly accomplished the effect of making the law well known, but it was very burdensome.

Penalties for noncompliance with the law are a two-hundred-dollar fine and/or 120 days in jail, and the law applies to everybody but those with a physical or mental disability which prevents them from safely operating a firearm, and those with conscientious objections based on their religious beliefs. Approximately 85 percent of our households already had a gun when the law was passed, and there was no organized opposition to the law, although a few citizens unsuccessfully attempted to organize against it. We were sued by the ACLU and by a private citizen who happened to be an attorney, but the ACLU bowed out of the case after determining that the law could not be set aside on constitutional grounds, and the other suit was dismissed on procedural grounds.

We are a growing community located on an expressway system that is twenty-five miles from downtown Atlanta, so before the law, we were getting some crime spillover, but not much. Our belief, however, is that any crime is too much. In the year before the law was passed, we had fifty-four residential burglaries and four armed robberies, both kinds of crime which we thought the law would affect. After the law, there were seventeen burglaries during the first year, and nine the following year, while in the two and a half years we've had the law in force, we have had only one armed robbery. We don't know of any variable other than the gun law which would account for those figures.

Also, along with the law we instituted firearms-safety training programs with both classroom instruction and training on the firing range. A high percentage of our citizens have completed those courses successfully, and there have been no firearms-related accidents or firearms-related homicides since the law went into effect.

I know that our law seems to have been effective in reducing crime, but I don't know what effect the antihandgun laws in other communities have had. I do, however, find it interesting that in Morton Grove, the best known of those communities, public officials are exempted from the handgun ban. I read recently that the mayor's wife got herself a handgun and ran into some sort of legal trouble about how she obtained it, and I found that interesting, too.

"I like everybody, but when somebody tries to kill me . . ."

VIRGINIA VELASQUEZ *owns and operates two adjoining stores in the East New York section of Brooklyn. She received a National Rifle Association cash award for foiling an attempted robbery in February 1983.*

About three weeks ago, two men came in here. One of them had two guns, and he pointed them at my watchmaker. My watchmaker said, "Oh my God, it's a holdup!" and he started running through into the other store. I started running, too, but something came into my head, and I got my gun, and I ran through the other store and out onto the street and back to the front door of the jewelry store.

One man was taking the jewelry, and the other was holding the guns. The man with the guns turned around and pointed them at me. He tried to shoot, but the gun he tried to shoot was old, and it didn't work. No bullet came out. I figured my life came before his life, so I started shooting. I shot five times and hit him twice in the head. Maybe I hit the other guy in the chest; I don't know. The first guy fell down, then got up and ran down the street, bleeding, with his guns. The Housing Police found him, and came here and said, "You had any trouble here?"

I said, "Yes. Why?" They said they had a guy hurt, and they brought him here, and I told them he was the one.

They told me later that one bullet grazed his head, and the other one went in and came out again. He had a very strong head. When they took the X rays, they found out that he still had some shotgun pellets in his head from a holdup he'd done before. He was twenty-six years old, and he was on parole when he came to hold me up. They didn't catch the other guy.

I was held up before. Jesus Christ, I don't remember, but it was about four or five times. One time, a guy came in with a shotgun. When I saw it was a shotgun, I ran.

I've had the gun about a year and a half. Before that, we didn't have a license. My husband has a big gun, but he's not here when they do the holdups, so he got me the little gun. He taught me how to hold it, but I never shot it before I shot the guy. Now I'm going to the pistol range twice a week. I want to learn how to shoot well. It's nice. I enjoy it. It's good to learn, especially in this neighborhood. I like everybody, but when somebody tries to kill me . . .

We've been here fourteen years, but it wasn't always bad. It started to get bad about six or eight years ago. Maybe it's going to get better. They're fixing up buildings and building new ones. My husband and I are going to retire to Puerto Rico in five or six years, and build a mall in our home town. It will cost about $250,000. It will be very nice.

When I got the award, I was very happy. I was proud. But I never tried to kill anybody. I tried to scare them and defend my life. God decides who is killed.

"He folded up his knife and walked away."

GEORGE KAST *has been a private investigator in New York City for twenty years. He carries a two-inch-barrel .38 Special revolver. He has removed the grips from the gun's handle in order to make it less conspicuous in his pocket.*

I always wanted to do this job. I guess I saw *The Maltese Falcon* when I was a kid, and just decided I wanted to be a private investigator more than anything. I've worked for an insurance company for twenty years, but I also do outside work for various attorneys, mainly tracking down witnesses and getting them into court. Every case is slightly different, and I like meeting all kinds of people and conning them into coming in to trial.

You don't get a pistol carry permit with the job; you have to get that separately. I got mine when I thought I would have some accounts that would want an armed guard. As a matter of fact, the first job I thought I'd need it for was a job protecting some visitors who were coming to the city. The thing didn't materialize. One of the people got killed, as it turned out, so I was glad I didn't get the job.

I usually carry the gun when I'm out working, and I don't mind having it in the house, either. What I like about it is that it is sort of an equalizer. I don't think I'd be much of a match for some big tough guy without it.

It's comforting to know the thing is around. I was with a friend one night, and some guy came along the street and bumped into him, and they exchanged a few words. The guy pulled a knife on him and announced that he was going to stick him. So I felt very happy to have the thing at the time, because I took it out and pointed it at him and told him he'd better not. He folded up his knife and walked away. And going into a rough neighborhood with surly people around who mutter at you, it's more reassuring to have something there. It's more or less saying, "Well, I'm as big a guy as you are."

I carried it most zealously when I was looking for the guys who murdered my aunt a couple of years ago. She was done in by some animals up in the Bronx. She was an old lady who remained there, one of the two old ladies who stayed on the block. There was a rash of "push-in" robberies: these idiots like to push in the door on old people who are returning from shopping or something. These guys thought that was a great way to spend time. They beat her up and left her there all night, and she died in the hospital. There was a witness to it, so what I did was ride around the neighborhood with the witness, looking for them. Apprehending them with the weapon would have been a lot easier than simply asking them if they wouldn't mind coming along with me.

The cops got them in the end. There were about ninety crimes attributed to them. They caught one guy on a roof. I told them, "Why didn't you just push him off? Why bother with this fuckin' beast?"

I've got a friend I listen to who's found a new three-dollar bullet that I carry in the gun. I use it because it'll destroy what it hits. I think if you're going to shoot somebody, you don't just want to scare them.

"It was on every bullet he used, like a mark."

DETECTIVE GEORGE SIMMONS *has had thirty years of experience in the NYPD ballistics lab, the largest and busiest in the United States.*

Here in the city you can't buy handguns or handgun ammunition legally, so what we get most here at the lab are shotguns and .22s; they can buy that ammo, so they cut the shotguns down and use the .22s in pistols. We get quite a lot of black powder guns, too, and BB guns by the hundred. Military guns, too—.45s and 9-millimeters galore—'cause you have people in the service who swipe the ammunition. Even shotgun and .22 ammunition comes from the military. You get a guy from the military who gets a box of ammo—he can sell it for ten dollars here and take his girlfriend out. Of all the stuff we get, though, the black powder guns are the worst. They blow up. I don't like 'em, and I hate taking pieces of gun out of my skull; it bothers me.

We are able to make matches—to prove that a certain bullet was fired from a certain gun—in 75 to 80 percent of our cases, but we do have limits. Shotguns are hard to match, for instance, because their barrels have no rifling and they fire multiple pellets; unless we have the empty shell case or we can match the wad from the shell to the gun—which we can only do when somebody's sawed off the barrel and left marks which show up on the wad—we don't have much to work with. Bullets that are very badly deformed don't give us much to work with, either, and then you get problems with guns that have been in sea air or been misused or cleaned with a stainless steel brush since the crime. The interior surface of the barrel and the breech face and all may have changed.

A lot of it comes down to experience. Me, for instance, I'd been looking at bullets almost thirty years when I got the Son of Sam case, so I knew exactly what kind of gun they should be looking for by the third shooting. I'd seen those markings on .44 Special bullets before. I said, "You're looking for a Bulldog."

Everybody said I was crazy, but I hit it right on the head. I said, "No, that's a Charter Arms Bulldog, .44 Special." The rifling on the bullets was a right six twist, and it was peculiar, and I knew that that was because of the way Charter Arms makes barrels for that gun. They bore the barrels in twenty-four-inch lengths, and when they bore them, one end is clamped and the other is free. It vibrates, and as the cutter gets toward the end it starts to make a different impression. That was the little peculiarity about some Bulldogs, and it was on every bullet he used, like a mark.

That was a hard case. The gun wasn't in good shape, so the matches were hard. There were a lot of bullets, too. I'd be digging them out of things, out there at four o'clock in the morning. We don't go out of the office on cases—Crime Scene does that these days—but they got me out of bed for that one. I tell you, I'm glad they got him when they did; that day, they were sending me down tests on fifteen hundred Charter Arms Bulldogs collected from New York State.

That was something. He said the devil sent him, in the form of a dog. I went up to his apartment. The only things in it were a hi-fi, a mattress on the floor, and the chair the hi-fi was on. That was it. And he had a hole in the wall—"Put Sam's messages in here" written there. Nobody reached in the wall; we could hear a scurrying going back and forth in there.

"I knew as much as the police ballistics man did."

DAVID BREITBART *is a successful New York criminal attorney known for his defense of underworld figures such as Harlem drug lord Nicky Barnes. He carries a 9-millimeter CZ-75 pistol, and is a competition shooter.*

Having a lot of knowledge of guns because I'm a shooter is, of course, to my advantage in court. I've won a lot of cases simply by knowing the characteristics and capabilities of weapons and proving that the prosecution's scenario couldn't have happened the way they said it did.

I had one case, for example, where the deceased had seven bullet wounds. The government took the position that my client was the only perpetrator and the only shooter. They had a problem, though: they hadn't found any empty shell cases at the scene, so they were saying that my client had used a revolver, which does not eject cases as it fires. A revolver, however, fires only five or six shots before it has to be reloaded, so the government explained the seven bullet entry wounds by saying that one of the bullets had hit the deceased in the hand before hitting him in the face.

This was a fallacious premise, just post hoc reasoning to justify the original reasoning, but the ballistics expert took the stand and testified to it. In fact, it was obvious to me that the face and hand wounds were made by separate bullets simply because the entry wound in the face was smaller than the one in the hand, and there was no way that a bullet could have gone through the man's hand and gotten smaller. The deceased had in fact been shot with three guns, and the witnesses were lying.

In that case, my knowledge of comparative bullet diameters and velocities and the concepts of terminal ballistics and expansion characteristics was instrumental in convincing the jury that the witnesses had not seen what they said they did. I knew as much as the police ballistics man did, and I proved my case through him, and it was so convincing that the jury ended up rewarding me with an instantaneous verdict.

The presentation of that kind of evidence by the prosecution is a common occurrence in the criminal justice system. Many times I have been exposed to situations where police officers lied, intentionally attempted to either frame somebody or embellish the evidence. The funny part of it —if you can ever be humorous when talking about people's lives—is that they usually frame guilty people by embellishing evidence, and by so doing they create the outlets for lawyers like myself to get an acquittal.

Knowing guns and being facile in the terminology is of great benefit to me in dealing with physical evidence, then, and there's an ancillary psychological benefit, too: most cops take a very macho, physical approach—"I'm a cop, a tough guy"—and if you know more about his thing than he does, it gives you a tremendous psychological edge in every area of cross-examination. This guy has the image in society of a weapons expert, but the average cop really isn't, and to be shown up not to be the macho man of the image really blows it for him. I do that all the time.

That helps me, but I am very disheartened by the peace officers I see. They really shouldn't be as ignorant as they are.

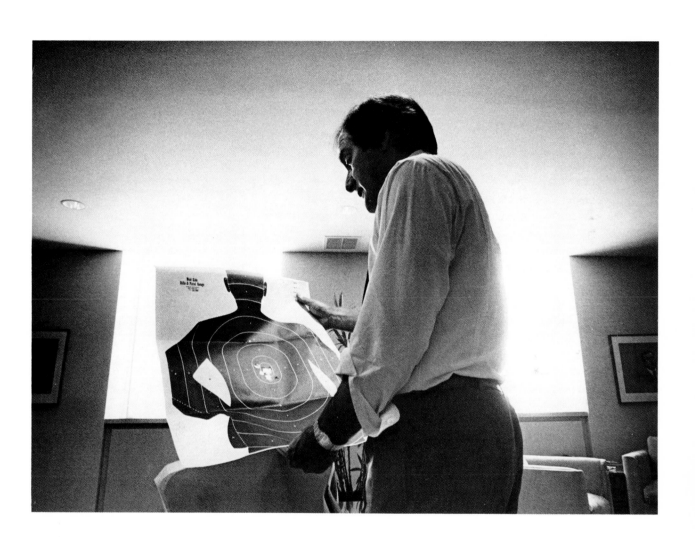

"I knew it right there and then: I knew I was dead."

DETECTIVE JOHN SNIDERSICH *of the New York City Police Department's Street Crime Unit was southbound on Broadway with his partner, Kevin Shea, when he heard a shotgun blast and saw a cloud of banknotes billowing into the midtown Manhattan street.*

I saw an individual going down into the subway. When I got to the subway entrance, he was coming out the other side, and as he walked out he nonchalantly bent down and started picking up money and putting it into his pocket. It had been in a paper bag in front of his shotgun when he fired at one of the bank staff, and he'd blown it all over the street.

I came up behind him till I was about seven feet away from him. I was dressed like a street person, with long hair —I looked like I was off to the races—but I had my shield exposed on my chest, hanging from a leather thong around my neck that Kevin had made for me.

I told the guy who I was, and to put his hands up in the air, turn around and take it easy. With that he just looked over his shoulder back at me.

It's funny. Sometimes you look at certain people, and their eyes are vacant, and you know: there's no personality behind this individual, he's all drained of emotions. As he turned around, I saw the .38 in his hand.

I told him that if he put the gun down I wouldn't kill him, that it was all right, nobody was hurt so far—and with that he just turned and fired several times at me. I returned fire, and we had a little dance right there and then.

He ran parallel to the building line, and I ran with him. Then he turned and fired again at me. I fired back at him again. Then he hit me three times—once in the arm, once in the belly, where it hit a Marine Corps belt buckle that I had on, and once in the sternum, right in the center of my chest.

Physically, it was like getting hit in the chest with a sledgehammer. It hurt a lot, and it was hot. Emotionally, I just knew right then that I'd never see my wife or my son again. I knew it right there and then: I knew I was dead. When the bullet hit my chest there was this burst of blood, like a mist, and there was a sound. There's a lousy sound— you can't describe it.

I knew I was dead, then—there was a hole the size of a quarter in my chest, and I was bleeding like a bastard—but I was damned if I was going to go out with that bastard standing in front of me. He was still there and still armed, and I was going to chase him. That's the way I felt it was supposed to be.

I fired my last round at the guy, then ran right after Kevin, who was running after the guy. I went down just around the corner, then got up again and started to reload, but then some other cops approached me and wanted to take me to the hospital. Thus began the ride of my life, but that's another story.

It turned out that it wasn't all over; the round had hit the key ring connecting my shield to the thong, then ricocheted into my sternum. If the shield hadn't been there, the bullet would probably have severed my spinal cord at that range. As it was, it just fucked me up completely for a couple of months.

Kevin caught up with the guy and had to shoot him. They brought him into the same emergency room I was in at Bellevue, but he didn't make it. His bullet's still in me, between my rib and my lung, and it hurts like a sonofabitch. One bad thing about it is that now it's too uncomfortable for me to wear a bulletproof vest.

"I personally have been shot thirteen times with a 9-millimeter."

BEN JONES *is a machinist and gunsmith, an IPSC competition shooter, and a professional soldier whose past affiliations include the U.S. Army Rangers and the French Foreign Legion.*

Given the choice of any weapons for my personal use in combat, I would start with the .45 Colt Government Model for my pistol. That's because of the gun's effectiveness as a man-stopper and its ability to function under severe conditions of dirt and weather. I'm not going to tell you that a 9-millimeter won't get the job done—there have been millions of people all over the world dispatched with one—but I personally have been shot thirteen times with a 9-millimeter, and it didn't do me in; as a matter of fact, my adversary didn't live through it. He used a submachine gun from no more than ten feet away, but he just never hit any vital organs. I killed him with a knife. Now I'd hate like hell to think about getting shot thirteen times with a .45.

Professional soldiers, given a choice, will choose a .45 almost invariably provided that there's adequate ammunition, which there usually is in any area of the world where the United States is or has been a presence. Sometimes that isn't the case, though, and you have to use something else; I've used plenty of 9-millimeters in my time. You also have to keep in mind that whatever weapon you use, you have to be able to get spare parts for it. You can't carry a broken weapon around for two or three months, hoping to find parts for it. That's why in Central America, my choice of a submachine gun would probably be a German MP-40 or MP-38, the old "Schmeisser." There are plenty of 'em around in that part of the world, and they're still good weapons.

For a rifle, I would choose the Belgian F.N.-FAL in .308. Of all the military arms there are in the world today—and there are some pretty good arms lying around—this particular weapon is the Cadillac. It's real accurate, it's as near mechanically perfect as you can get, it will take the abuse that an old M-1 Garand will take, it'll function under almost any conditions and with ammunition that would hang up in any other kind of automatic weapon, and it has extreme range and fine handling qualities. Those Belgians are an ingenious bunch, and the F.N.-FAL is one of the most sought-after weapons in the world, by any group.

You don't see too many of them in the hands of "rebels" because they're so expensive. The government forces usually get them under military aid programs, and of course the rebels will go to great lengths to capture one of them. They won't buy them, though: you have to remember that these people don't have any money—they're patriots fighting just for survival—and they're a lot more interested in supplying large numbers of weapons than just getting a few great ones. They can get six or seven or even ten Soviet or Chinese AKs for the price of an F.N., and those are effective weapons. The anti-Soviet forces in Afghanistan are using Chinese AKs supplied through an arrangement between us and the Chinese Government, and they're doing a fantastic job with them.

Personally, I'm not restricted in my choice of weapons when I go down to Central America. Arsenals are available to me, so I choose the F.N. and a compensated, worked-over .45 like the one I use in IPSC shooting at home. That's no "trick gun": I wouldn't shoot a weapon in the game that I wouldn't put my life on in combat.

"If they hit the ground with their legs crossed, they're dead."

PARIS THEODORE *is a weapons designer formerly employed by the U.S. Government on classified and covert weapons projects. He is pictured in his Manhattan office working on his self-designed "guttersnipe" pistol sight. In the background is a target for his QUELL system of combat handgun shooting.*

Hollywood has been responsible for most errant ideas about combat and what actually happens in a shootout. Television and the movies mislead and misinform us regarding combat, and like so many six-year-olds sitting before our TV sets (for that, indeed, is what we were), we absorbed that information like sponges. For the man who will never be engaged in combat, no problem: what he does not know will not hurt him—but many of us went on to become police officers, agents, and even training officers, and we carried those Hollywood lessons with us. For those of us who chose that path, there is a danger: when "it" really happens and the adversary does not follow the script, we become confused. This is because we have been brainwashed to a degree any KGB political officer would gloat over.

From the movies, we have learned to expect that when someone is shot in the arm, he reacts immediately by grabbing it with his free hand, wincing, and maybe uttering an "Unh!" When he is shot in the chest, a spot of blood appears and he is thrown backward, usually with arms flailing, to land motionless and silent.

The truth of the matter is that no bullet from a sidearm, no matter what the caliber, will bowl a man over. The "stopping power" or striking force of the bullet can have no more impact than the recoil of the gun: otherwise, the man pulling the trigger would be bowled over, because as every high school senior knows, every action is accompanied by a reaction of equal force in the opposite direction.

The striking force of a modern .44 Magnum throwing a 240-grain ball at a muzzle velocity of 1,470 feet per second —almost twice that of a 1911 .45 Colt semi-automatic— would strike a stationary two hundred-pound man at arm's length with one twentieth the force of another man walking into him.

Also, one must remember that bullet wounds from a handgun are self-sealing and very rarely begin to show blood until moments after the crucial confrontation. And with very few exceptions, a bullet entering the body causes no immediate pain and cannot be felt entering.

A member of the old NYPD Stakeout Unit once told us, "If they hit the ground with their legs crossed, they're dead. No further shooting of that felon is required. Go on to the next one." As fate would have it, this has proven to be an excellent rule-of-thumb. Crime scene unit personnel and shooters seem to concur on this point in hindsight. Nobody has ever seen a man who fell crosslegged stand again. The feeling is that a man who lands like that has been neutralized on his feet.

One must never make the mistake of taking a cue from either the opponent's facial expressions or words—which historically have been used deceptively—and one cannot believe in "knock-down power." The closest thing to it in combat is a "cadaver reaction" or a nervous spasm, both of which happen when the brain fires a confused barrage of synapses simultaneously when the opponent is shot (or possibly even when he thinks he is about to be shot). That can make a person scream, twitch, jump, or defecate, but it has no bearing on the number of foot-pounds of energy just delivered by a bullet.

I conceived of the QUELL system of combat handgun shooting to address these realities.

"The kill zones are the spinal column, the mouth area, and the kidneys."

STEVE BLIZZARD *left the cast of the TV soap opera "One Life to Live" in order to run a gun-safety program for actors. He is a ranked expert with combat handguns, and has been demonstrating Paris Theodore's patented QUELL system to police departments around the country.*

The QUELL system of combat shooting is highly realistic. It leads to greatly increased accuracy and a much higher percentage of hits which will disable an adversary.

The stance is the first element. Over the years, there have been a variety of shooting stances, but the QUELL stance is one of those simple, logical ideas just waiting for somebody to realize it, and it works far better than any of the others.

The key to it is that the shooter uses his left eye, not his right, as the dominant eye in sighting. That is because the left eye appears to give a more objective view of the situation than the right, which means that you are more likely to place your shots more accurately. With the subjective vision of the right eye, emotion under fire appears to be more likely and you are more liable to "freak." This is a purely experiential observation, but it holds true in most people: the left eye works better under stress.

In the QUELL stance, then, you shoot double-handed, and you cock your head across and down onto your extended arm, sighting with your left eye. That stance improves your accuracy immediately; it certainly improved mine, and it has worked with all the people I know who have tried it.

The other part of the QUELL system is hit effectiveness. The overall objective in a shootout is to terminate the action of your opponent, but the question is, when is that action terminated?

The answer is that it is only terminated when your opponent has collapsed and landed crosslegged, or become separated from his weapon. If he is not in that position and he still has his weapon, you have to assume that he is still a threat.

This is where the QUELL target comes in. On the target the "kill zones" are the spinal column, the mouth area, and the kidneys—nowhere else. That's because the only ways to stop a person cold are to disconnect the central nervous system or lower the blood pressure instantaneously. Hits to the spinal column or the medulla oblongata—that's the mouth area—short-circuit the central nervous system, while hits to the renal arteries—the kidney area—immediately lower blood pressure. The QUELL targets, therefore, are life-sized photographs of armed opponents in various positions relative to the shooter, and the shooter must aim for where the kidneys, spinal column, or lower face are in that position. The areas are marked on the back of the target so the shooter can check his hits.

You see, the whole system of combat shooting today, the objective of which is "center of mass" shots to the heart and lung area, is a throwback to trophy-hunting practices. The objective there is to preserve the trophy head, and in most cases it doesn't matter if the animal isn't *immediately* killed or disabled. That, of course, is not so in a shootout with an armed and dangerous opponent: then, it matters very much that a person can take a hit in the heart and still keep coming at you. That's happened time and time again in combat, when people often don't realize that they've been shot. The wound may be fatal within minutes or even seconds, but during that time the opponent can still kill you. Without a central nervous system or blood pressure, he can't.

4232-3
5-03